The Toad Prince

LACY WILLIAMS

THE COWBOY FAIRYTALES SERIES

6

THE TOAD PRINCE

CHAPTER ONE

Five-point-two miles from home.

She'd been planning her big escape from her small life for twelve months and two days, and she'd only made it five-point-two miles from her home in north-central Texas.

All her careful planning, all the scrimping and saving, down the drain.

McKenna Hastings took two steps back from the open hood of her battered twenty-year-old pickup and stared at the steam rising from the engine. The truck made an ugly roadside decoration against the bright blue sky and fields green with their spring growth.

She'd spent years working on the truck. Changed the oil, the spark plugs, the battery, even the alternator, once.

She knew her truck. And she knew this had been coming, had hoped and prayed that the truck's last legs would hold for just a while longer.

Apparently, she'd long ago used up her last wish.

She'd already checked on Maximus. Her horse seemed content standing in the trailer attached to the truck. He wasn't shaken at all, not like she was when she'd seen the steam pouring from beneath the hood. The April weather was mild, and he'd be fine in the trailer until she came up with a solution.

Tears threatened and she valiantly sniffed, trying to stem them.

A few slipped free, and she swiped at them with the backs of her hands.

Her three cousins were going to laugh so hard when she had to call them to tow Maximus back home.

They'd already made every joke they could think of about her quest to become a rodeo queen.

This was supposed to be the first leg of her journey. The first event was tonight. She'd imagined Mama and Daddy looking down from heaven, watching and smiling on her. She was going to redeem Daddy's tragedy, live up to Mama's legacy on the circuit.

She touched the locket beneath the neck of her T-shirt. How could she give up now, when she was so close?

An engine revved and then idled. She swiped at her tears again, in case it was someone she knew—no doubt the small town grapevine would quickly catch wind of her failed adventure.

She turned to see an unfamiliar black truck, a current-year model if she wasn't mistaken. With boosted wheels and silver rims that sparkled in the midmorning light.

It rolled to a stop on the two-lane road beside her

broken-down pickup.

The passenger side window lowered with a smooth electric slide—she was hit with a little pang of jealousy for her truck's crank windows—to reveal a handsome dark-haired man she'd never seen before.

"Need some help?" he asked in a barely-there accent she didn't recognize.

"Maybe."

She might only be nineteen, but she knew better than to get in a vehicle with a total stranger. On the other hand, she had grown up with three male cousins and knew how to fight her way out of almost any situation.

And a huge part of her was trying to find a way—any way—to keep her dream from going up in a puff of smoke.

Maybe it was foolish, but she stepped closer to the truck and stood on tiptoe to see inside. "I don't suppose you have a spare six-cylinder in here anywhere."

She used the moment to get a good look at her would-be hero. Wow, he was handsome. He had piercing blue eyes and a patrician nose. She'd read that in a book once but had never seen anyone who fit the description, until now. His strong jaw was covered in a day's worth of dark stubble.

Broad, muscled shoulders stretched beneath a plaid-patterned shirt complete with silver snaps up the front and on the pockets. The shirt didn't appear to have ever been worn before, and neither did the dark stonewashed Wranglers that encased a muscled pair of thighs.

She couldn't see his feet but would almost bet that his boots would be brand-new, too.

His outfit made her think he was some kind of would-be cowboy. The interior of his truck was spotless. No signs of anything a real cowboy would have on hand. Not a pair of leather gloves, a horse's hoof pick, or a coil of rope or anything else.

Maybe he was a serial killer posing as a cowboy, out looking for unsuspecting young women. Ones who wouldn't know any better.

"Are you quite finished checking me out?"

Her head snapped up, and she caught the end of his smile, one that invited all kinds of trouble.

And that was enough to make her step back from the truck.

A shadow moved deep in his eyes. Then he slid on a pair of designer sunglasses with dark lenses, hiding the nuances of his expression from her.

"Do you need a ride to town? Isn't there a little hamlet just up ahead?"

"A hamlet?" she repeated. She'd never heard anybody use that term outside of a romance novel.

Who was this guy?

No one could call the podunk hole she was trying to crawl out of a "hamlet."

"Town's three miles that way." She jerked her thumb over her shoulder. "But I'm not going there. I'm on my way to Austin." She slanted a look back at the rusted white trailer. "I can't leave my horse.

Maximus is worth ten times more than my truck was."

* * *

Prince Pieter of Glorvaird couldn't believe the girl he'd stumbled upon.

Oh, he could easily agree that the horse she claimed was worth more than the truck would be without even seeing the animal—the pile of junk that still had steam rising from beneath its hood had obviously seen better days. Probably during Pieter's childhood.

But what he couldn't understand was why a beautiful woman like her was out here towing a horse trailer alone. With her sandy-colored long hair streaming down her back and dancing hazel eyes, and those features... She could easily be a fashion model.

And she was *young*. She couldn't be more than twenty. Her fresh-faced demeanor and the naivety coming off her in waves made him want to warn her off. She might as well wear a target on her back for unsavory people.

People like him.

Not that he had the time or the head space to devote to anything else right now. He was on a mission.

He wasn't even sure why he'd stopped.

Or why the sight of the silvery tears she'd tried to wipe away affected him. He wasn't one to be affected by a woman's manipulations—not after dealing with his mother since his childhood.

The girl seemed suspicious of him, which he supposed was a good thing. It was novel that she didn't recognize him as a prince. In Regis, where he and his mother made their home, he was well known and recognized often.

Was it providence that she was stranded here when he, too, was driving to Austin?

He'd landed in Dallas and traveled to the small town where the newspapers reported his cousin, Alessandra, lived while in the United States with her fiancé, a rancher. He'd arrived only to find his cousin gone to some cowboy competition—a rodeo— several hours away. Too far away to enact the revenge that drove him.

His mother spoke often and fondly of her growing-up years spent in Glorvaird, but she spoke even more of being betrayed by his uncle, the king, and forced out of her beloved homeland.

Wasn't Pieter a son of Glorvaird? Didn't he deserve to be embraced by the homeland he'd never visited? He didn't hold out hope for any kind of reconciliation with the royal family. He'd come to Texas with a vague idea of finding the one thing that would hurt his cousin the most.

The crown had abandoned him. The king was his uncle, yet he'd never met the man. Certainly he and Henri could've used some guidance over the years on how to deal with his mentally ill mother.

As far as he was concerned, his cousins and the king deserved what was coming to them. He just had to find the perfect vehicle for delivering the revenge he desired.

He'd never met his cousin. The papers reported she'd almost died, thanks to his mother's assassination attempt. The stories of her devoted fiancé, a former solider, claimed he was very protective of his soon-to-be bride.

Would it be easier to approach Alessandra if Pieter arrived at the rodeo grounds with this young woman? Who would ever suspect someone as innocent-looking as she?

He didn't know what her business was in Austin. Perhaps there was a chance she was going to the rodeo, as well, since she was towing her horse. Not that it mattered. He knew how to woo a woman to his way of thinking, and they'd have several hours in the truck together for him to win her over.

"It happens that I am also on my way to Austin," he said. "To meet my cousin."

A shadow of something—perhaps suspicion—flitted through her eyes, though she hid it quickly. Good girl.

"Perhaps we could strike a bargain."

She looked over her shoulder to the trailer. He saw the fine lines at the corner of her eyes as she considered his offer.

It wasn't as if there was much traffic on this two-lane road. No one had driven past during the several minutes he'd been stopped here.

She bit her lip, and he knew he'd won. She was going to agree.

"I'll tow your trailer and your horse to Austin. But what will you give me?"

She leveled a flat gaze on him, mouth firmed in a line. "Not what you're thinking, I'm sure. I'd rather call my cousins"—the deep frown she wore when she mentioned them told him how much she didn't like the idea—"than get physical with you."

He laughed at her unexpected words. Usually women were content to ply their wiles on him, try to charm him. But not this country girl, with her jeans and T-shirt and hair in a braid down her back.

Her frank words were such a complete departure from what he was accustomed to that his smile lingered.

And only seemed to increase her suspicion.

"I'm serious," she said.

He leaned his elbow on the steering wheel, body turned almost completely toward her now. "I can tell."

"So you... aren't interested?" He couldn't get an accurate read on her expression. Was she relieved or disappointed?

He couldn't say it without lying, not after what she'd just stirred in him. "I didn't say that," he returned. "But I think I can control myself for the four or five hours it takes to get you to Austin. Will you come along, then?"

"You said we'd strike a bargain." Her chin came up, and he clamped his lips against the urge to smile again. She might give a good show of trying to be tough, but he'd had so many hours of reading his mother that it was really more adorable than anything else.

"A boon then," he said. "To be redeemed later." It was almost too easy. He'd find a way to use this girl to get close to Alessandra.

She looked back again, and this time he realized she wasn't looking at the trailer, but at the road. Was she running away from something?

He reminded himself that he didn't care.

"It's a deal." She stuck her hand through the open truck window, and he stretched out to shake it. He was surprised by how calloused it was—almost what he might expect from a working *man's* hand.

"I'm McKenna Hastings."

"Pieter." He didn't give his title. Didn't want it getting out who he really was and what he was doing here, not until he'd formulated a better plan.

"I'll get Maximus out of the trailer," she said. "It'll be easier to unhitch that way."

He pulled his truck into the drainage ditch in front of hers, just in case someone did meander down this road. The truck was a rental and a high-dollar one at that.

By the time he'd gotten out of the truck, she'd fitted a ramp to the back of the open trailer and was backing out a magnificent solid black gelding.

He wasn't a horseman, didn't know much about conformation or the value of the animal, but he could see she'd been right about the animal's worth. It was almost comical, the juxtaposition between the quality of the animal and that of her vehicle.

It certainly made him curious.

The shiny black boots he'd purchased at a store in Dallas pinched his toes as he crunched through the grass at the road's edge.

He peered down at the connector where the trailer was hooked to her truck. He had staff that usually made sure his bicycle was attached to his sports utility vehicle when he went riding. And no idea how to disconnect this.

Then McKenna was beside him. "Here," she said.

He backed out of her way as she made quick work of untangling a chain and some wires and then lifting the trailer above the ball.

She was a slight thing, but she put her shoulder into the trailer and started pushing before he realized what she was doing.

"Hey!"

The trailer had already shifted by a foot or more before he joined her on the opposite side of the hitch and put his back into it.

The stupid boots slipped on the grass and gravel, and he almost lost his footing, but thankfully McKenna didn't seem to notice.

When they'd moved it several feet away from her truck and angled it so that he could back up to it, she straightened. She didn't even seem winded, so he tried to stifle his labored breathing.

"You move trailers by yourself often, Supergirl? I thought you said you had cousins to help you."

She shrugged, flicking a strand of hair that had fallen out of her braid and into her eyes. "A girl's gotta do what a girl's gotta do."

It was an answer designed to put him off, and he let it, for now. There'd be plenty of time to talk on the road.

* * *

After she'd hitched the horse trailer to Pieter's truck and loaded Maximus back inside, McKenna ducked into her pickup to grab her bags.

The canvas duffel and well-used garment bag might not look like much, but they held her dreams.

She looked around the inside of the truck she'd bought secondhand at seventeen. The county might tow it by the time she returned after the weekend was over.

Then she spent several moments sending a text to her best friend, Kylie. Her friend might be off having the time of her life at Oklahoma University, but they talked every day. McKenna raised the phone to snap a photo of Pieter's truck, another of the man himself, and typed in his license plate number, since she'd been up close and personal with it while she'd hooked up the trailer.

She might be taking a chance accepting a ride from a total stranger, but she couldn't let this setback ruin her one chance at scholarship money that could change her life. And there was no way she was going with Pieter without leaving a trail of breadcrumbs for her friend, just in case.

Then she took a deep breath and got out of her

truck. She was going to be in a world of trouble when one of her cousins drove to town and saw the abandoned truck. Would they think she'd been abducted?

But she still didn't text or call them. She would later. *Much* later.

She couldn't risk them coming after her and ruining her chance. They'd already done enough with their jeering and joking.

Duffel in hand and the garment bag slung over her shoulder, McKenna approached the black truck.

She'd known Pieter was a city boy pretending to be a cowboy based on his clothing, and his actions since he'd stepped out of the truck only confirmed her initial impression.

A real cowboy would've known how to unhitch a trailer. Would've known not to wear dress boots to work outside—or in her case, push a trailer. And a real cowboy would've followed her to her truck, asking if he could carry her bags.

There weren't cowboy *rules* so much as a code of honor.

And Pieter most definitely didn't have it.

Which made her wonder just why he'd stopped to help. She'd seen the calculation in his eyes. Knew that his "boon" might be painful when it came due. But she really had no choice, now did she?

Her new friend sat in the driver's seat adjusting the stereo as she opened the passenger door and then the rear door so she could load her bags into the backseat. It really was a nice truck, lots of legroom back there.

"You okay?" he asked, shooting a glance at her.

"Fine." She didn't need a man to open doors for her or unhitch her trailer. After her mom's death when she was three, she and her dad had made due. He'd taught her independence early on, told her Mama'd had an independent spirit.

Then when he'd passed, too, in the middle of a storm of disasters, she'd been thrown into life with her aunt and uncle and cousins. She'd had to lean on that independent spirit often, just to survive her abrasive, often rude and bullying cousins.

She'd learned fast to keep quiet and stay out of the way. She could do for herself.

All she had to do was prove herself.

Pieter put the truck in gear and eased onto the road.

She felt the slight rocking of the truck that meant Maximus had shifted in his trailer. In her truck with its bad shocks, she could feel every movement the horse made, but in this new model truck, the thousand-pound animal shifting barely caused a blip.

Her new friend glanced in the rearview mirror. "Anything I should know about pulling a horse trailer?"

"Max is a seasoned traveler," she said. "But horses sometimes move around. You shouldn't have any issues with this baby and its towing capacity, though." She patted the leather seat next to her thigh. The car even smelled new.

She couldn't help watching his hands flex and

move on the steering wheel. He had nice hands. Powerful hands. Even if they were a bit soft, like she imagined a banker or stockbroker would have. Someone who worked inside, at a desk job.

Her cell phone pinged a message tone, and she glanced at it as unobtrusively as she could.

Kylie: OMG girl you're crazy! At least he's a hot stranger...

Pieter glanced over at her. "Your family?"

"A friend. I sent her your picture and your license plate number. Just in case you're a crazy serial killer."

He grinned, eyes back on the road.

Was it her, or was his grin particularly feral-looking?

He tapped his index finger against the top of the steering wheel. "So...what's your story? Runaway?"

She wrinkled her nose, turning to stare out the window. "No," she said smartly. "I'm a competitor."

"Traveling alone?"

She shrugged. "My family is busy." And they weren't invited anyway.

"What event? Tub racing?"

Brows furrowed, she glanced at him. "Oh, you mean barrel racing? I'm guessing you've never been to a rodeo before..."

"Good guess. Then barrel racing, is it?"

"No." Her face heated and the words stuck in her throat. She had to clear it once before speaking again. "I'm competing to be rodeo queen."

She waited for his chuckle or even a smirk. She'd gotten enough of that from her cousins. But it didn't come, only a curious sidelong glance. "That's more like a pageant, isn't it?"

"Yes."

She'd won the local rodeo queen title last summer. That's when her plans had really started taking shape. How many times had her cousins told her that she was only good for her appearance?

So why shouldn't she use her looks?

Kylie had supported her plans to enter this larger competition in Austin, though McKenna's best friend didn't know the depths of desperation she felt to escape her life.

But McKenna had a niggling worry that the hometown title had been a fluke. What did she really have to offer to the larger rodeo community?

She needed the scholarship money if she was going to get out of her minimum wage job as a grocery store checker. Since her tenth birthday, she'd dreamed of being an attorney, a better one than her father's.

She couldn't give up now.

CHAPTER TWO

Gideon Hale strode through the outdoor rodeo grounds in full mission-planning mode. Early afternoon sunlight warmed his head and shoulders, though a brisk breeze ruffled his hair.

The former Navy SEAL had agreed to this plan of Alessandra's, but that was before he'd seen this venue.

His contacts had turned up a lead on the lost princess of Glorvaird, Alessandra's half sister, and they'd come to Austin to try and meet up with her at the rodeo.

The fairgrounds were a nightmare. Right now, they were fairly empty. The rodeo queen competition would begin tonight, and several RVs and horse trailers had parked in the venue's large lot, but the dirt-packed arena and other fairground buildings were empty and quiet.

He imagined them filled with cowboys and cowgirls, moms and dads and kids. Most of the people attending the rodeo would be here for the fun and the competition.

But if somewhere were here with evil intentions...

Well, there were too many places to hide. Nooks and crannies between buildings. Even rooftops, where a sniper could have easy access.

The fairgrounds were impossible to secure, even with a larger force than the hired security team he'd assembled.

And he was dreading going back to the upscale Austin hotel and telling Alessandra that he didn't want her out here in the open.

After the huge engagement ball they'd hosted back home had gone off without a hitch, and after five months with no further credible threats, Alessandra seemed to believe that the target was off her back.

He wished he could be so sure, but his time in the military had taught him that threats rarely ever just *went away*. They might go dormant for a period.

But they always came back.

And it was his job to protect her. She'd nearly died on his watch, and he'd vowed never to let that happen again.

The problem was that Alessandra had recently learned about her half sister, the product of an illicit affair of her father's, and she was determined to meet the girl and bring her back to Glorvaird before the king died. With their upcoming wedding—a huge shindig that would take place in a Glorvaird cathedral with five hundred attendees—only six weeks away, Alessandra seemed even more determined to locate the princess *now*.

The missing princess had a last known residence in the States but had dropped off the map until recently. His contacts had turned up a barrel racer on the rodeo circuit who matched the age and birth date of the missing princess.

They still weren't one hundred percent sure this Tara Ballard was the princess they were looking for. It would take a DNA test to confirm her true identity, but Alessandra refused to be placated or to let Gideon handle the issue.

Alessandra had some kind of idea that if she saw this girl, she'd instantly know whether or not it was her long-lost sister.

He'd tried to caution her about getting her hopes up. Tried to tell her that the other woman might not want to connect, that there might be a reason she'd fallen off the map.

But nothing would stop his fiancée's optimistic hopes.

He'd promised to try. And he would.

But his first priority would always be Alessandra's safety. So how could he convince her to stay away from the rodeo over the next week?

* * *

Pieter couldn't contain his curiosity about his passenger as he drove the truck southwest along a flat, straight two-lane highway.

A rodeo queen.

He'd met plenty of models and actresses, had even dated a couple.

McKenna just didn't seem the type. Oh, she was

pretty enough. Striking even, with her elfin features and bright eyes.

In his experience, women who were interested in pageants and modeling were usually vapid, extremely interested in fashion and money—his money—and self-absorbed.

And yeah, he'd only just met her, but he sensed that McKenna was more hometown girl than anything else.

So what was her deal?

"How'd you get into pageanting?" he asked. "Was your mother a rodeo queen or something?"

She was still staring out her window, and he couldn't take his eyes off the road for very long, but a sidelong glance at her revealed a wistful expression crossing her face.

"Yes. A long time ago. Last summer one of my cousins entered me in a local queen competition as a joke. But I went through with it and won. So…now I'm here."

There had to be more to it than that. He knew there must be. But she didn't seem to want to say more.

She set her chin again and looked his way. "What about you? What business do you have in Austin? You're obviously not a native Texan."

His shoulders wanted to tense, but he'd had many years of practice in hiding his true feelings, so he merely tightened his grip on the steering wheel and forced a smile he didn't feel. "I'm actually heading to the rodeo, as well. I'm meeting someone."

From the corner of his eye, he saw the tilt of her head. Felt her glance. "Hmm."

That was it. She *hmmed*.

"Is it a surprise? For the person you're meeting?" she asked.

He shrugged. "Sort of." Alessandra wouldn't be expecting him. He couldn't be sure whether she even knew he existed.

"Then you might want to reconsider your clothes."

He looked down at himself briefly. "What's wrong with them?"

"You don't look anything like a genuine cowboy. You'll stand out for sure when surrounded by real Texas good 'ol boys."

"How does a real cowboy dress?" he asked wryly. They'd only just met and she was critiquing his attire?

"Mostly T-shirts and jeans. But your jeans are so starched and clean, they've obviously never been worn before. And your boots..."

The continuous pinch of his toes made him cranky as he asked, "The boots?"

"They're dress boots. For Sunday church or maybe a fancy date night. Not for every day."

He stifled the growl that wanted to rise from his throat. She was dressed much like she'd described, her braid flipped over one shoulder of her T-shirt. Her boots were worn leather and caked with dirt and he didn't want to know what else.

"You should've asked the salesperson for help," she said. A small smirk played around the corners of her lips.

"I was in a hurry"

"To meet your cousin." She slanted a glance at him.

She was ether too nosy or too smart for her own good.

"Tell me more about this pageant of yours." He gave her a charming smile, one that usually worked to distract or disarm.

Before she could answer, her phone rang.

She sighed deeply but clicked the line open and held the phone to her ear.

"Where the heck are you?" came a belligerent male voice, loud in the quiet cab of the truck.

She must've accidentally opened the line on speakerphone.

Was this one of her cousins? A boyfriend?

She moved the phone away from her ear with a wince. Her focus moved to the phone's screen as she tapped rapidly, probably trying to silence it. "Hey, Todd."

"Where are you?'"

"I'm on my way to Austin. You already knew that."

"Then why is your truck sitting on the side of the road?"

She grimaced as she kept punching at the phone, but there must've been some error because she didn't raise it to her ear again, and it remained on speaker.

"McKenna!"

He didn't know her family dynamic, but the

person on the other end of the line was pushy. Of course, Pieter'd had his own doubts about her being on her own and broken down on the side of the road. Could he blame the guy for being a little protective?

"The engine finally fizzled," she said as she glanced out the passenger window. "But I caught a ride."

"With who?"

She shot a furtive look at him. "A friend."

"What *friend*? And why didn't you call me?"

She mumbled something beneath her breath. "I didn't call you, or Taylor, or Andy, because I already knew what you would say."

Great diversion. She'd completely ignored the question.

"What, to stop being stupid and just come home?"

Ouch. There was a difference between protective and outright rude.

McKenna's face had turned crimson, and Pieter found himself wanting to defend her.

Which was crazy, because he didn't have the time or inclination to get involved. It wasn't his problem. *She* wasn't his problem.

"Look," the voice came through the phone. "The rodeo queen thing was a great joke, but you're never going to win at a big rodeo like the one down in Austin. Why don't you just tell me where you are and I'll come get you?"

Pearly white teeth emerged as she worried her bottom lip. Her blush had faded some. Her brows were furrowed, and she looked like she was considering this idiot's words.

"Why don't you tell him to get lost?" Pieter whispered.

"Who was that?" Todd's voice boomed over the speaker.

McKenna shot Pieter a glance. He couldn't tell if it was annoyed or grateful. "I told you, I got a ride."

Before her cousin could demand to know more, she rushed on. "I'm going to Austin, like I planned—"

"You're never going to win—"

"I'll be back in a week." She hung up the phone.

An uncomfortable silence fell.

"You might want to power it off," Pieter offered helpfully. "Your family isn't very supportive, are they?"

* * *

McKenna stifled a bitter laugh.

Unsupportive was an understatement.

"My aunt and uncle are my guardians," she said slowly, not sure how much she really wanted to tell Pieter—a virtual stranger—about her family. On the other hand, everyone around town knew her story, so why not him? It wouldn't change anything.

"They're…fine with me going down to Austin." It was a bit of a stretch. The truth was, they really didn't care as long as she was out of their way. "It's my cousins—three of them, all older—who can be controlling."

Controlling was a kind way to put it. They'd bullied her throughout her childhood and teens. Now that she was older, they mostly threatened and teased her.

She desperately wanted to move out of the house, but working a minimum wage job meant she couldn't afford it.

"How'd you end up with your aunt and uncle?" Pieter asked.

She glanced out the window, her hand creeping up to touch her locket beneath her shirt.

"My mom died—I can't even remember her, I was so little. For a while it was just me and my dad. Then he…" The words stuck in her throat, a hard knob of emotion even after almost a decade.

Even if everyone in town knew—or thought they knew—what had happened, she hated talking about it. Her father had been wrongly accused of committing fraud through his financial services business. He'd been jailed and been assigned a court-appointed attorney, who'd botched the case.

Her father hadn't lasted three months in prison.

"He died when I was ten," she said, because she couldn't tell the rest. "My aunt and uncle took me in."

And she'd been thankful, but sometimes it was hard. Sometimes she felt like excess baggage, like they'd be just as happy without her there.

"Sounds like it was hard on you. How old are you, anyway?"

Her chin went up at the slight challenge in his

question. "Old enough."

His raised eyebrows told her he wasn't going to let it go. "Seventeen?"

"*Nine*teen," she shot back. Old enough to be on her own, if she could just afford it...

"Nineteen," he muttered under his breath, shaking his head a little.

"Why does it matter?" she asked. "How old are you? Thirty?" She threw out the number because she wanted to irritate him right back, but she pegged him closer to twenty-five.

He smirked a little. "Older than you. Wiser, too. Do I need to be worried about these cousins coming after me with a shotgun?"

"No. Probably not," she amended. Even though Todd had called to berate her, she doubted he or his brothers could be bothered to drive all the way to Austin.

"You don't sound very sure."

She couldn't tell whether he was teasing her or not. She didn't want to talk about her cousins any more. They loved to tell her that her looks were the only thing special about her and that she'd wind up some man's housewife, barefoot and pregnant because she'd never make anything of herself.

Kylie had been the only person in her life who'd told her anything different. Kylie believed McKenna could be criminal defense attorney, something she'd dreamed about since her father's botched trial. She never wanted another family to experience what she had.

Pieter slanted a glance her direction. "So your cousins entered you into the competition but now they don't think you can win?"

"They entered me as a *joke*," she reminded him. "I'm not exactly a fashion icon or anything. Horsemanship is my strongest suit."

Her cousins had hooted and howled from the stands when she'd walked onto the makeshift runway for the fashion portion of the contest back home. She'd visited the attic and found her old gun used for bedazzling clothing from elementary school and gone to town on a boot-length denim skirt she'd found at the nearest Goodwill two years ago. She'd found a sparkly pattern surfing the web at the public library.

She'd also spent hours poring over videos that showed different riding patterns for the horsemanship part of the competition. Not to mention the questions for the interview with the judges.

She wasn't poised. Wasn't confident. Had no idea what she was walking into.

The cash winnings from the small-town rodeo was a windfall she'd never had before, and she'd plugged the money into fancy duds for the fashion part of the Austin competition.

She was betting everything on this. College tuition was expensive, especially if she wanted to make it all the way to law school.

"There's a big difference in our small-town rodeo and what you'll see in Austin. Austin is a regional rodeo that pulls more riders"—and queen contestants—"and the competition will be much tougher."

Another one of those slanted glances. "You're pretty enough to win. What are you so afraid of?"

Her face went hot at his compliment.

Suddenly, there was a loud *pop,* and the steering wheel jerked to the right.

Blowout!

She grabbed the door, her seatbelt locking tight against her chest as the truck bucked, fighting the trailer's weight from behind and the loss of momentum.

Pieter gritted his teeth as he worked to guide the truck toward the shoulder.

Finally, they rolled to a stop. A semi zoomed past, stirring a cloud of gravel dust that swirled past the truck.

She panted, trying to control the racing of her heart.

"Are you all right?" Pieter asked. His face was white.

"Yeah. I've got to check on Maximus."

She could only pray her horse wasn't hurt.

What would she do if she got to the rodeo and didn't have a horse for the contest?

CHAPTER THREE

Maximus was unhurt but agitated as McKenna slipped through the trailer beside him. He neighed and bobbed his head, showing his displeasure at the sudden and shaky stop.

"Easy, boy," she said, rubbing one hand against his neck to settle him.

She checked both front legs, but he didn't appear to have lost his balance or kicked any part of the trailer, which might've injured him.

She sighed, tears threatening because of her relief.

"All right," she told the horse. "I'm going to go see how quick we can get back on the road."

Outside the truck, Pieter stared at the blown front tire. It was completely shredded. They weren't driving anywhere on it.

"Know how to change a tire?" she asked, already guessing the answer.

"I know how to ring for a tow," he said, still staring at the tire.

She sighed. "Not necessary. I can do it. Let me unload Maximus, again"—she muttered under her breath—"and I'll change the tire."

"Isn't it dangerous to do that right off the side of the interstate?"

As if to underscore his words, a sports car blared its horn as it passed them, going well over the posted speed limit.

She glanced at her watch. "I'm supposed to check in for my interview with the competition judges in five hours. If we wait for someone else to do it and then have any other delays, I'll miss it completely."

And she couldn't miss her one shot.

"Are you certain?"

She nodded. She couldn't quit now.

She unloaded Maximus, who wasn't happy about the noise coming from the cars passing on the interstate. This particular field that they'd stopped near wasn't fenced, and there were no nearby trees, so there was nowhere to tie him off.

"You're going to have to hold his lead," she told Pieter, who'd stood back to let her work.

Pieter approached her at the horse's head, well back from the interstate.

"I'm not, ah..."

"You don't like horses?" she asked.

"I'd prefer to ride a bicycle," he said. "I'm an avid cyclist."

It figured.

"Well, for right now, you're going to be a real cowboy."

She gave a quick introduction to Maximus, letting the horse get his scent. "Just act confident." Pieter shouldn't have any trouble with that, not with the cocky smiles he'd been delivering. "He'll be able to smell if you're frightened."

And the last thing she needed was for her horse to bolt along this stretch of interstate.

Pieter grudgingly took the lead rope.

She glanced over her shoulder as she trudged toward the truck to see man and horse sizing each other up. "Don't stare straight at him!" she called back.

"Are you sure you won't need help?" Pieter returned.

She only shook her head and kept going.

It took longer than she wanted. She ended up having to unhitch the trailer completely to get at the spare tire connected beneath the truck bed.

It was heavy work that made her arms and back ache and, at one point, she ended up lying on the ground on her back to get the jack positioned correctly.

She got a blister cranking the lug wrench, but at last, after almost forty-five minutes of sweaty work, she had the tire back on and the trailer re-hitched.

She couldn't wait to get back in the air conditioned cab.

She blew hair that had come loose from her braid off her forehead as she walked toward Pieter and Maximus on the slight hill off the side of the highway.

The horse munched on summer grasses while the man sat with legs outstretched. He got to his feet as she approached. He offered her Max's lead rope, and she took it, grimacing at the black oil on her hand against the white rope.

"Thank you," she said.

"Thank *you*."

She wrinkled her brow at him.

"For fixing the tire."

She waited for more. Waited for him to say something snarky, like one of her cousins would. He just stared at her.

She wiped at her cheek with the back of one hand—the only place that seemed remotely clean—and hoped she hadn't smudged oil on her face. "Aren't you going to ask if it's safe to drive on?"

His brows creased. "Why would I ask that? I just watched you change the tire."

"Yeah but…"

He still seemed puzzled.

"I'm a girl. I'm not as strong as a man…" She heard her cousins' voices, even though the words came from her own mouth.

She shook her head, turning to the truck and trailer. She wanted in that A/C now. Especially with her face flaming so badly. "Never mind. It doesn't matter."

"Hang on." He caught up to her, tugged on her elbow. For once, his gaze was clear and sincere. It stopped her in her tracks.

"Do you let your cousins feed you that load of crap? Because I've just been watching you work your butt off and thinking that you'd never trust your horse to the truck if you didn't feel it was safe."

That was true. So was his assumption that it was her cousins' voices she heard in her head. She'd heard the refrain that she wasn't good enough daily.

* * *

Pieter gazed down at the pixie of a woman and her too-wide eyes. She wore a slightly skeptical expression, but he didn't have to look far to see the slight vulnerability revealed beneath.

She really didn't know how impressive it was that she'd just manhandled that truck tire into submission?

"You've got a smudge..." He pointed to the bridge of her nose.

When she lifted her oil-stained hand, the one not holding onto the horse, he caught her wrist. "You'll make it worse."

He reached up himself, carefully brushed away the dust with his thumb.

Nineteen. She was only nineteen.

He repeated the words internally, needing them to cut through the waves of attraction that battered him.

She was practically a baby.

He was only twenty-four, but after dealing with his mother since his childhood, along with the expectations of being nearly royalty, he often felt much older. Hadn't he seen the worst in people over and over again?

She was not his type, he reminded himself, but he seemed to be caught in the laser-beam of her bright-eyed gaze.

His hand moved to cup her cheek.

And then it was knocked away as her horse butted its head between them with a *whuffle* of breath.

"Maximus!" She didn't sound particularly upset, though, as she curled her arm beneath the animal's neck and turned her face into its coat. She'd probably welcomed the intrusion.

Pieter stepped back, exhaling heavily.

He didn't even know where that spike of attraction had come from. She wasn't his type. She was too naive and fresh-faced. He'd destroy her if he let her get too close.

He moved to the front of the truck as she loaded her horse in the trailer. His phone rang. The display showed it was the mental health institution where Mother resided. He let the call roll to voicemail. He'd deal with it later.

As he slid into the cab and cranked the engine, he felt the weight of the ring on his right pinkie.

McKenna's face appeared in the passenger window. She opened the door.

He flipped on the A/C. He'd noticed the fine sheen of sweat across her brow and upper lip—he'd been too close—and she needed to cool off.

They both did.

* * *

Pieter had talked McKenna into stopping off at a combination gas station and mom-and-pop diner, even though she'd told him it wasn't necessary.

She was worried about getting to Austin in time, but he was hungry and knew she must be too.

He owed her for fixing the tire, at the very least.

He came out of the washroom to find she'd already cleaned up, removing the last traces of oil from her hands and arms and fixing her braid.

She sat in a small booth, half hidden behind a rack of garish postcards.

He watched for a long moment as she bent over something, reading silently and then mouthing something to herself. Flash cards?

She started to stand when she caught sight of him approaching, but he motioned her to keep her seat.

"We should get something to eat. You might not have time to grab supper before your event tonight."

She started to shake her head, and he couldn't help but wonder if her protest had more to do with her wallet than her appetite. He quickly rushed on. "My treat, since you saved me from paying a tow company."

She still looked like she might protest, so he slid into the booth next to her, effectively trapping her in her seat.

A harried-looking waitress in a stained apron over a worn knee-length uniform rushed over. She stopped short and gave him an assessing gaze. Grinned at him. "What can I get for you, hun?"

He started to order a grilled chicken salad when he caught McKenna's slight shake of her head.

"Always get the special," she whispered to him,

then proceeded to order just that—a bacon double cheeseburger with fries and a chocolate shake.

"Roadside diner etiquette?" he asked when the waitress had moved on.

"Common sense. Not many people come to places like this to order a salad, so you can count on their vegetables being old and wilty."

Smart thinking.

He leaned his elbow on the edge of the table, propped his head on it, and craned his neck to get a closer look at the index cards she had spread on the table.

"*Who is the rodeo commissioner?*" he read aloud.

She slapped one palm down over the cards and shuffled them into a pile. "I was just reviewing some questions they might ask me tonight."

He raised one brow at her. "So who is the commissioner?"

She gave a name he didn't recognize, and she must have been right, since she'd been practicing, but with her head ducked down, her voice was just a mumble.

"You'll never make a good impression talking to the table—or to your hands."

Her shoulders straightened. "I was just *practicing answers.*"

He shrugged. "Seems if you're going to practice, you should do it right. Hand over the cards."

He moved into the opposite side of the booth, so she was forced to look at him.

She hesitated, her hands covering the cards on the tabletop.

"Come on. I won't poke fun at you."

She looked up, watching his face. For what, he didn't know, but he met her gaze squarely.

Finally, she pushed the stack of cards across the table.

He shuffled through them and chose one at random. "Define *jackpot*."

She explained how the rodeo winnings worked, speaking almost in a monotone.

He looked back down at the cards in his hands. "Do you want the truth?"

She nodded tightly.

"You sound a little...wooden. Rehearsed. You should be more natural when you answer, if you can."

She bit her lip, the third time he'd seen her do that. Was it her nervous tell? "How? If I'm nervous just sitting here with you, how do I pretend that I'm not when I'm in front of a judge?"

He made her nervous. Did she feel the same attraction that had seemed to spark to life between them?

If so, he was in trouble. He had only so much goodness in him, and he'd already used up a lion's share when he hadn't leaned forward and kissed her next to the truck.

"Think about your best friend," he suggested. "Pretend you're talking to her instead of to the judge."

She nodded slowly, a smile dawning across her lips.

And that made his stomach flip.

He returned his gaze to the card and asked her about the current head of the PRCA. This time she was slightly more relaxed.

He watched her for long, silent moments after she finished. Mostly to see what she'd do when she became uncomfortable.

Noise from the patrons around them intruded. Snatches of conversations, clinking silverware, a muffled shout from someone in the kitchen.

She held his gaze steadily, then a slow flush climbed into her cheeks. Her eyes flashed.

"What?" she hissed across the table. "It was the right answer."

He nodded. "I know. I just wanted to see if you'd lose your composure."

Her face mottled again, but he couldn't allow himself to feel sorry for her. "No matter what, you must maintain your composure."

It was a hard lesson. One he'd learned first at his mother's knee, then later when the press speculated on his connection—or lack thereof—to the royal family, sometimes even getting in his face about it.

She looked to the side. She breathed in and out, her shoulders rising and falling. She was so easy to read. Which intrigued him all the more. He was unused to women who showed their every thought and feeling so freely. McKenna was a breath of fresh air.

He glanced at the next card but didn't read from it. "Don't you think it's cruel to the animals they use in the rodeo events? The steers and bulls?"

"That question isn't on the cards."

"Are you going to sass the judge like that if they ask you something you don't want to answer?"

She frowned at him slightly, but he wiggled his eyebrows at her, challenging her. "There will be questions where they aren't looking for your memorized answer. They'll want to know what *you* think."

Her eyes slid past him as she gave the question thought.

"There are a lot of protections for the animals," she said slowly, "both in and out of the arena. And I guess I don't see how it's any different than breeding animals for human consumption. So no, I don't think it's cruel to use the bulls or steers for rodeos."

"That was your best answer yet."

She beamed at him, her obvious joy hitting him low in his stomach. Didn't anyone ever tell her *good job?*

Thankfully, the waitress appeared with their artery-clogging meals, providing a much-needed interruption and another of those looks.

McKenna noticed, raising a brow at him, though she didn't comment.

After the waitress left, McKenna dug in, chomping through the burger and stuffing herself with fries. Another refreshing change from what he was used to, as most women he dated ordered salads and ate daintily. Not this one.

He sipped the chocolate shake, letting the sweet

coldness flow over his tongue.

She swallowed. "It's good, isn't it?"

"You were right." He was glad he'd let her change his order.

She beamed again.

How in the heck did this woman let her cousins walk all over her, tell her she was worthless? How could she believe them?

And what was he doing, trying to use her to get close to Alessandra? The next bite of burger tasted like ash in in his mouth.

He'd wanted revenge for so long that he couldn't imagine letting it go. He wanted his cousin to feel some of the same pain he'd felt at being abandoned by his family and left to the manipulations of his mother. It was incredibly difficult dealing with a parent who was mentally unstable on his own.

For so long, revenge had been the only thing he'd wanted. How could he even sit across from someone as pure and sweet as McKenna and not poison her?

Should he just forget about the boon entirely? He could easily drop off McKenna and her horse at the fairgrounds and go on his way. That would be better for her, but he wasn't willing to let her go just yet.

CHAPTER FOUR

Orange light from the setting sun filtered through the open drapes in the hotel suite Alessandra shared with Gideon in a posh Austin hotel. She sat on the sofa in the living area between the two bedrooms, idly paging through a bridal magazine. In the background, the TV flickered as it played a national news station, but she'd muted the volume an hour ago.

The magazine was mostly a guise to hide her nervousness. Most of the wedding preparations had already been put in place. She'd hesitated to even come over to the states with Gideon, as the wedding was only weeks away. And her father's health had declined much in the past months. Now he had trouble eating and speaking. Often when he allowed her to spend time with him, he listened as she read or they sat in companionable silence.

She hadn't been able to stay in Glorvaird knowing that Gideon's people had a strong lead on her missing half sister. Plus, she hadn't wanted to be away from her fiancé, and he had to visit his family's ranch and tie up some loose ends before they returned overseas.

Gideon had agreed that they would remain in Glorvaird after the wedding. Everyone tiptoed around the subject, but her father was not long for this world.

The sound of a keycard being inserted into the door brought her head up from the magazine. The door opened, revealing Gideon.

Alessandra jumped up from the sofa, leaving behind the bridal magazine.

He took off his Stetson and set it on a credenza near the door, giving her his shoulder momentarily. The tense set of his back wasn't a good sign.

She slid her arms around his neck and squeezed, giving him a *welcome home* peck on the lips, hoping to erase some of the tension.

It didn't work. The tight muscles of his shoulders and neck didn't relax at all.

"I ordered room service," she told him. "A nice juicy steak and baked potato for you."

It was one of his favorite meals, but his expression didn't reveal an iota of peace. He nodded. "Thanks, Allie-girl."

She let him go, and he sat in the sofa she'd just vacated. She perched on it next to him.

"Obviously, you have bad news. Why don't you just tell me?"

He flicked a glance at her. "The fairgrounds are a security nightmare. There's no way to control who comes into the venue. On top of that, there will be trucks and trailers in and out all day. Even with a team surrounding you at all times..." He sighed. "I don't like it."

"All right."

His head jerked as he looked at her. "What?"

"I said, *all right.*"

He shook his head slightly. "I heard you, but…
All right, you're fine with the risk, or *all right*, you'll
stay at the hotel?"

"I'll stay here."

She shouldn't laugh, but she couldn't help a huff
of soft laughter at his stunned expression. "Do you
want me to argue?"

"No. I just…thought you would."

She scooted closer to him and put her arm around
his broad shoulders. "We're getting married in less
than a month. That means I trust you with my life. If
you don't think it's safe to be out at the rodeo, then
we'll make other arrangements. Find some way to get
Cindy"—the barrel racer they'd come to meet with—
"to come here."

She wasn't sure that Gideon's hunch that there
was still someone after her was right, but she wasn't
joking about trusting him with her life. If he didn't
want her out in the open, she could respect that.

Some of the tension left him, and he turned to
capture her lips in a searing kiss. "Thank you," he
whispered against her lips.

She hummed her *you're welcome* back to him
without breaking the kiss.

Finally drawing away moments later, he leaned his
forehead against hers. "Is it too late to elope, like
your sister did?"

She brushed a final kiss against his jaw. "That ship has sailed. You lost your chance when Mia got married."

He groaned low. "I know."

She thought he was mostly joking about calling off the royal wedding. It was too late now anyway, as the cathedral where her mother and father had been married was being prepared. The invitations had gone out weeks ago—to nearly five hundred guests—and her sisters would be her attendants, as was tradition.

She couldn't wait to be married to Gideon, but she also couldn't forget why they'd come here. "Maybe we can patch Mia in on the meeting with a video call. Do you think Cindy will mind?"

A tiny bit of tension returned to his shoulders. "We still aren't sure she's your sister."

She nodded. They hadn't been able to match up financial records, although they could always do a DNA test, though that could take weeks. But she was cautiously optimistic that this was the lead they'd been waiting for.

"When can we set up a meeting?" she asked.

He sighed again. "I'll reach out to her when she arrives tomorrow. If she is your half sister and she knows it, she may not be receptive."

Alessandra couldn't think about that. She had to keep hoping.

And then take her new sister home to say goodbye to their father.

* * *

Time had been tight when they'd hit traffic in Austin, but they'd made it to the fairgrounds with an hour to spare before McKenna's interview. She'd been here once as a small child and the venue still seemed as huge as it had back then with its stock barn, show barn and outdoor arenas. Could she really win at an event this big?

After the fiasco of her broken down truck, she hadn't had time yet to form a new plan and knew that Pieter planned to check into a hotel later.

She had no funds for that. She'd planned to bunk down at one of the cheap hotels near the fairgrounds—if she could find an available room at this late date—but now she needed to find a way home. She couldn't count on winnings from this rodeo, and who knows how much money it would take to get her horse home. She needed to conserve what little cash she had left.

She didn't have time to worry about where she'd sleep tonight. Right now, she had to face this interview. She found a public restroom and washed up as best she could, dressed in the slim, dark wash jeans and dress boots she'd bought for the occasion. She wetted her hair down in the sink and dried it with her hair dryer, then put it up in rollers and sprayed it with copious amounts of hair spray. Hopefully that would battle through the humidity in the air tonight.

Then she donned the glittery black snap shirt she'd chosen for the occasion. She focused on keeping her breathing even and deep. Ran through the instructions Pieter had given her. *Pretend the judge is Kylie. Breathe deeply. Keep composure. Think.*

She didn't understand him. Pieter had spent nearly an hour, at lunch and then on the road, coaching her. As if he'd had media training himself or at least been in the public eye often. She still didn't know anything about him.

Except that she'd thought he might kiss her back beside the interstate.

And she wasn't sure how she felt about that. Her cousins had often told her that her looks, her body, were the only things men would be interested in.

She'd been very careful not to put herself in a position that would prove her cousins right. She hadn't gone to prom. Hadn't ever been in the backseat of some teenage boy's car.

She'd never even been kissed.

And she had the sense that Pieter was a player. A rogue. That he had experience—a lot of it. Someone like him would probably laugh at someone as inexperienced as she was, thinking that he'd wanted a kiss.

She yearned to be valued for more than just her appearance.

She did the best she could with the makeup—she rarely wore any, and without a mom around, didn't know what she was doing—and took her hair down, spraying it again with the aerosol hairspray.

She'd left her black felt hat in the truck and needed to put her duffel back. The cooling evening air had her taking a deep breath, though it did little to calm her jangling nerves.

When she hit the gravel parking lot, Pieter was there.

He took one look at her and then a double-take. "What'd you do to your makeup?"

Her stomach flipped at his question and the horrified expression on his face.

"What?" Her face went hot, but she hid it as she opened the passenger door and tossed her duffel onto the front seat, then ducked around the open door to lean down and look at her face again in the side-view mirror.

"You've…" He rounded the front of the truck, moving toward her and shaking his head. "You can't go to the interview like that."

Was it that bad? She didn't think she looked like a clown or anything. "I did the best I could."

"Wasn't there any other woman in there who could've helped you?"

She shook her head. She'd been alone in the public restroom and knew that most of the other queen competitors were likely getting ready in hotel rooms or travel trailers. Besides, who would want to help a nobody like her, anyway?

"It's too late—" she started, but he shook his head almost violently.

"Do you have one of those makeup-remover wipes? Maybe we can fix this."

She did, though she had to dig through the duffel to get to the package.

"Where's your makeup bag?"

Seriously? He was going to do her makeup?

She guessed it was no more of a role reversal than her changing the tire on his truck. She motioned to the duffel—there wasn't anything she was ashamed of in there—and he pulled out the gallon-sized plastic zipper bag stuffed with the remnants of makeup she'd collected during her teen years.

She'd never purchased makeup for herself. When you were dirt poor, even the cheap drugstore stuff was out of range.

So when girls at school would leave the ends of their eyeshadow or blush in the bathroom, she'd take it. She wasn't proud of it, and it probably wasn't the most sanitary thing, but it was what it was.

She hardly ever wore it anyway.

But she saw the furrow of his brow as he looked through the odds and ends.

She scrubbed at her face with the wipe and pretended she didn't care.

* * *

"So you've done this before?"

Shadows fell around them as Pieter fought to keep his focus on the tiny eyeshadow brush he was wielding and not the smooth face beneath his fingertips. From this close, McKenna's lush lips were a distraction he could ill afford. Each breath she took warmed the skin of his chin and jaw.

"No," he admitted. "But I've watched."

He'd smeared plenty of lipstick before and

watched as dates had reapplied their makeup. Sometimes on large wall-mounted mirrors. Sometimes on small compact mirrors.

And anything had to be better than the job McKenna had done on herself. The colors hadn't been natural, the base washing out her complexion and the too-dark blush making her look like a vampire or something.

He finished applying the smoky gray color that made her eyes pop and went back to the plastic bag McKenna had given him with her makeup inside.

That had been eye-opening.

"So... This is an interesting collection of makeup for an aspiring rodeo queen."

Her eyes remained closed. "My family doesn't have a lot of money."

He'd guessed as much from the sorry state of her horse trailer and the dilapidated truck, but this was... He didn't purchase makeup obviously, but he didn't think it could cost that much, even for the department store brands. She seriously didn't even have a couple hundred bucks for something so important in a pageant?

He was beginning to think perhaps her aspirations to be a rodeo queen were a long shot. Wouldn't the other girls have the very best?

Not that McKenna didn't look hot in those slender jeans that showed off shapely legs and that black button-up shirt that sparkled with her every movement.

But she was all country girl. They'd be polished.

Unfortunately, there was nothing to be done about it now.

He tried to remind himself why he was here, that he shouldn't care about some waif he'd picked up on the roadside. He'd only given her a lift because he wanted the boon, hadn't he?

What did it matter if she failed in her little mission? He wouldn't see her again after this weekend.

Except it mattered to her. Couldn't forget the pinched expression on her face when she'd hung up on her cousin, or the determination she'd shown when he'd peppered her with questions over lunch.

"So how'd you end up with your horse?" he asked. "If your family isn't well off?"

Pieter didn't know anything about horses, but even he could see that the animal was quality. Tall with strong lines, and that glossy black hair...

"He was my dad's. Dad was a small-time farmer with big dreams of breeding horses."

She'd mentioned her dad briefly before, that he'd passed away, and Pieter couldn't help noticing the little catch in her voice.

"You should see him perform…"

Her voice trailed off, her eyelids fluttered open, and he was distracted by the depths of her eyes. It took him a moment to realize she was still talking about the horse and not her father.

"I mean, if you aren't busy tomorrow, the horsemanship competition is during the early afternoon."

Soft pink rose into her cheeks. He could almost feel the warmth beneath his fingertips as he smoothed out the blusher on her cheeks.

"I'm not sure I'll be around. I'm heading out to find a hotel in a bit." He let his hands fall away from her. Needed the distance. "Finished. You can do the lipstick yourself."

He tossed the blusher back into the plastic bag and held out the softer pink color than what she'd previously been wearing—a bright red that had clashed with her blush.

She bent slightly to see herself in the truck's side mirror. "Huh. You did a good job."

It certainly wasn't perfect, wouldn't stand up to the models he'd dated before, but it was much better than what she'd done.

She pursed her lips slightly, applying the lipstick quickly.

He moved another step back when she straightened, smacking her lips together lightly. "Thank you."

He nodded.

She put the lipstick back and turned away momentarily, then placed a black cowboy hat atop her head, completing her look.

She might not be perfect, but she was stunningly beautiful. If the judge was a male, no matter what age, he would have trouble concentrating on the event and not the woman.

"Okay," she said on a breathy exhale. She shook out her hands, and he couldn't help but notice her trembling.

"You'll be fantastic," he said, because it seemed like the right thing to say. And some small, long unused part of him wanted to comfort her in the face of her nervousness.

But instead of smiling back at him, her head tilted slightly to one side, and she seemed to be searching his face. There was no mistaking the hint of vulnerability in the depths of her eyes.

And, stupid him, he reached out and squeezed her hand briefly, the contact with her ice-cold digits a small shock. "I promise," he said, though he really couldn't promise any such thing.

But the slow smile that dawned across her face made him not care if his words were true. He'd do nearly anything to see that smile again.

CHAPTER FIVE

It was dark when McKenna returned to the fairgrounds parking area where Maximus's trailer remained, now unhooked from Pieter's truck.

There was movement inside the different RVs parked all around, muted voices from other queen contestants and rodeo competitors.

It made her feel a little lonely, trudging back to her horse trailer all alone. What would it be like if her mom had been alive? If she'd come along on McKenna's adventure? If she'd been waiting, ready to encourage her or mop up tears?

Or if her dad had still been here, cheering from the stands?

It was hard to imagine and a little silly to even think about. McKenna didn't need anyone waiting for her.

Good thing, too, because Pieter's truck was gone, just like he'd said. She hadn't expected him to stay, not really. He'd only come to the rodeo to meet up with his cousin, and somehow he'd taken her on as a little side project along the way.

She had to remember she still owed him a favor.

He wasn't being kind to her out of the goodness of his heart.

Hadn't her cousins taught her that men couldn't be trusted?

But even as these thoughts swirled through her mind, a flare of disappointment rose up. She was sorry that Pieter had gone.

She wanted to tell him that she'd aced the interview. She'd passed by two other competitors—both of whom had given her scathing once-overs before turning up their noses at her—on her way into the small room set aside for the interview. She'd seen their designer knee-length denim skirts, seen that their shirts were silk or satin or something much more expensive than hers, but she'd done what Pieter had suggested and pretended they didn't exist.

The judge, an older woman who looked like she'd probably seen pageant days herself, was kind and had seemed receptive to all of McKenna's answers. They talked for nearly an hour, and it had almost been like chatting with a real friend.

So much of McKenna's confidence had been a result of Pieter's parting words.

He believed in her.

He didn't even know her, but he believed she could do it.

She knew he was hiding something, knew that some of his motives might not be pure.

But she was drawn to him anyway.

She slipped into the horse trailer, stowed her hat and switched her boots for the sneakers she'd left there. Maximus was settled in the rented stall she'd reserved for him in the stock barn nearby. She'd checked on him on her way out here and found him sleeping peacefully.

She didn't like leaving him alone in an unfamiliar place with different sights and sounds than he'd have at home, but she also couldn't stand leaving him out in the trailer all night, small as it was. She needed him at his best tomorrow.

And what about herself?

She'd found the women's locker room, which did have a shower, so at least she'd present herself clean tomorrow.

If it hadn't died, she could've slept in her truck. It wouldn't have been the most comfortable of places, but...now it looked like it was the trailer floor. And the door didn't lock from the inside, which meant she was unprotected.

Not for the first time did she question if all this was worth it. At least living with her aunt and uncle, she had the security of a roof above her head, if not much else. Maybe she was dreaming too big, thinking she could be an attorney, could really help people.

She remembered those dark moments when she'd realized her father was never coming home. She didn't want that for another little girl. If this didn't work, she'd find another way to fund her education. But for now, she was stuck here.

There was nothing for it. She would have to make the best of it and pray that any dark circles that appeared on her skin wouldn't be too harsh tomorrow. She was purposely avoiding thinking about where she'd spend the night tomorrow. With rain in the forecast, the trailer would be soaked and miserable.

She changed out of the black button shirt, opting for a tank top beneath her sweatshirt—an oversized, beat up old thing that she loved—and curled up in a ball at the front end of the trailer. If no one knew she was in here, she'd be safe. Right?

But then a pair of headlights swept over her with a flash through the trailer slats. She shielded her head with her elbow, working to be as still and small as possible. Probably whoever that was would think she was some tack and wouldn't even look in the trailer.

The headlights cut off, but the truck remained idling.

Her heart sped. Even more so at the sound of a door slamming shut and boots crunching in gravel.

"McKenna?"

That was Pieter's voice. She didn't think she moved, but maybe she'd flinched when he'd said her name.

There was a creak of metal, then a flash of a light in her face. She winced and hid behind her elbow again, but he adjusted the light—his phone. He must be using a flashlight app.

"What are you doing in there?"

There was no use trying to hide now, so she stood and made her way out of the trailer. Her mind scrambled for some way to convince him to go on his merry way.

He took her elbow to help her as she stepped onto the pavement.

"I came back to see if you needed a ride to your hotel. What the heck are you doing curled up in the back of your trailer?"

She didn't have to answer for him to get it, because even in the low glare from the light post several cars away, she saw his eyes go dark.

But she didn't understand what he was angry about. A muscle ticked in his jaw, and he clamped her elbow. When he spoke, his accent seemed to thicken.

"Please tell me you weren't going to try and *sleep* in your *unlocked* trailer in the middle of this fairgrounds."

She heard echoes of her cousins' cruelty. *Stupid. Brainless. You'll never amount to anything.*

She jerked her chin up. "I'm an adult. I can stay here if I like."

"You're an adult. Then perhaps you should start *acting* like one."

His lips curled into a snarl, and she tried to wrench her arm away from his grip, but he held her too tightly.

"Let—" *Go.*

Before she could get the word out, his lips descended on hers with crushing intensity.

* * *

Pieter hadn't meant to kiss her.

He hadn't meant to let his emotions get the better of him. When was the last time that had happened? When he was thirteen and had gotten into a shouting match with Mother?

But now that he'd kissed McKenna, he found he couldn't stop with just one.

He'd meant the first kiss, not as a punishment, but an expression of the anger and the paralyzing fear he'd felt when he'd seen her and realized what she was doing, or trying to do.

But she'd frozen beneath his touch, both his lips and his hand at her elbow, and instead of continuing the punishing kiss, he softened his lips and pulled away slightly. Just far enough to brush butterfly-light kisses against the shadows of her eyelashes, one across her cheek before he returned to her lips.

This time, he started gently, teasing her lips until she responded, until she opened to him.

He used the hand at her elbow to draw her closer, let his opposite hand come up to cup the nape of her neck.

He didn't know why he found her so tempting. She was too young for him, he was too jaded for her.

But he couldn't stop what was blossoming between them. A big part of him didn't want to.

Then he pulled back slightly, intending to brush his fingers over the softness of her cheek before diving in to her addicting lips again.

But the few inches of distance gave him enough room to see the burning hurt and tears pooling in her eyes.

She pulled away from his hold. This time he let her go, but not without his stomach pitching as if he'd skydived off a skyscraper.

She turned and crossed her arms over her middle. As if to protect herself.

From him.

What had he done?

"Come back to my hotel room with me," he said. His voice emerged rougher than he'd intended. He'd booked the last room at the nearest hotel. The desk clerk had been talkative and told him twice how lucky he was.

McKenna shook her head almost violently. He saw her throat move as she swallowed.

Passion and confusion might be clouding his judgment, but he couldn't bear to see the hurt. He'd certainly not meant to put it there.

He closed his eyes against thoughts of her vulnerable, lying in that unguarded trailer all night. Alone. Defenseless. She was small, slight. Easy prey for someone with evil intentions. He couldn't stand it.

"I'm calling in my boon," he said before he'd really thought it through.

Her eyes flashed and her chin came up. "I already said I wouldn't sleep with you."

"I'll sleep on the floor." This time his voice was tinged with desperation. Something he'd never wanted to feel again. "Or in my truck. Just don't stay out here alone. Please."

He should've known that it would be the *please*

that did it, that got her to look at him again. She nodded slightly, quickly turning her face away again, though, before he could do more than see the tears still sparkling, unshed, in her eyes.

At least she'd agreed. Where she'd sleep was one less worry.

* * *

How exactly had he ended up here?

Pieter was a prince of Glorvaird. He'd never slept on the floor before in his life, except for those few awful nights during his childhood. He didn't like to think about those times. Ever.

But now he shifted on the uncomfortable thin carpet, a T-shirt and his sweatpants his only shield from the itchy fibers. His head rested on his bent elbow, and he stared up at the ceiling and the small red light that shone from the smoke detector. The pillow was missing half its stuffing and did nothing for him. Neither did the light blanket he'd found in the small hotel closet.

McKenna breathed deeply and evenly from the queen bed nearby. She'd wanted to refuse his offer to purchase supper. Maybe she didn't want to accept his charity, or maybe she didn't want to owe him.

He hadn't realized she was in such dire straits, even with the broken-down pickup and secondhand makeup bag. Should he have left her on the side of the road, instead of bringing her here? At least she'd been closer to family there, and surely one of her annoying cousins would've come and picked her up. Probably. Maybe.

He'd had to talk faster than ever before in his life to get her to accept a couple of slices of the pizza he'd bought from a fast food place on the way to the hotel. Surprising him again.

She'd practically inhaled the awful, cardboard tasting stuff, sitting cross-legged on the bedspread with no plate, only a paper towel in hand, watching television.

With her long hair spilling over her shoulders and her makeup all washed off, she looked like a teenager. But she'd kissed like a woman. Maybe an inexperienced woman, but he'd never felt such powerful emotion in a kiss.

Until she'd started *crying*. Had he frightened her? That certainly hadn't been his intention.

And what had been his intention?

No, he didn't want to go there, because he certainly hadn't been thinking, only reacting.

He couldn't tell whether McKenna had actually shed any tears, though, because she'd kept her face turned to the window the entire, silent ride to the hotel. She hadn't sniffled, hadn't wiped at her face, so he didn't *think* she'd cried, but she'd been close.

What had he been thinking, kissing her like that? He hadn't, obviously. He'd been turned upside-down, as if he'd taken a hard tumble from a fast-moving bicycle.

How had things gotten so terribly mixed up?

He'd lost his focus. He'd come to the States for

one reason only.

But somehow, from the moment he'd met her, his focus had shifted to McKenna and her troubles. Her innocence and her mission to win the pageant.

He tapped the fingers of his free hand in cadence against his chest. Then just his pinkie. His family crest ring was warm against his skin. Its weight reminded him of his purpose, reminded him that he hadn't checked in with the hospital. Probably his Mother had upset a nurse. It wouldn't be the first time, and he didn't feel a particular urgency to call. It could wait until morning.

Ah, Mother. All the reminder he needed that he couldn't afford to be tied up with McKenna.

He could never forget the little eight-year-old boy he'd once been, an innocent child, locked in the pitch-black closet of his mother's suite of rooms. Just the once, just one night. She'd put him there in a fit of temper.

When she'd let him out the next morning, she'd been all apologies and tears until he said he forgave her. But saying the words aloud didn't necessarily make them true, did it?

Because he still remembered the awful fear of being alone in the dark, remembered screaming until he'd gone hoarse, remembered banging on the closet door, praying she'd come back.

But she didn't come back.

And he remembered curling into a ball, shedding silent tears because he wanted a *normal* mother. Not one who sometimes lived in her own head for weeks at a time. Not one who forgot important dates, like when she was supposed to deliver him to his boarding school. One who forgot his birthday. Not one who cared nothing if he ate or starved.

And not one who maintained delusions of grandeur, imagining that she deserved the crown herself.

All he'd wanted was one person who loved him. Someone to take care of him.

And he'd been so resentful of the cousins that Mother had told him about. The ones who had a mother *and* father. Who never had to fear for their lives.

Where had they been all this time? Living in their Glorvaird castle.

When *he'd* needed someone.

Fury and resentment boiled through his veins, igniting the dormant emotion that had spiked next to McKenna's trailer. He'd stuffed away the desperate fear and anger at her carelessness in his effort to protect her.

He'd make a bank withdrawal tomorrow, that's what he'd do. He'd force McKenna to take some cash—or, if she absolutely refused, he'd hide it on her person. Then he'd wash his hands of her. She wasn't his problem.

And he didn't want to have to see that fear in her eyes.

It was like looking into a mirror from his childhood, one he'd ached to escape for so long.

He couldn't bear it again.

CHAPTER SIX

McKenna had slept hard and woken with her left arm asleep—a sign she hadn't moved in hours.

The hotel room was empty, sunlight streaming through a crack in the blinds. Pieter had left a short note on the dresser saying he'd had to run an errand and would return shortly.

And she was a little glad. She didn't know how to deal with the crazy emotions that the night before had made her feel as if she'd been bucked from a bull.

Her first kiss. And boy, what a kiss it was. She'd never imagined that kissing someone could feel like that. Like she was competing in a barrel race, adrenaline skyrocketing, galloping horseback flat out, the wind in her face. And how could somebody feel all that and as if they were spinning at the same time? No wonder she was all jumbled up.

She'd felt... like she'd mattered to him.

But she hadn't been able to quiet her thoughts and one important question: *why* had he kissed her?

Because she'd made him angry? Or because he wanted something from her? Because he certainly hadn't kissed her because she mattered to him. How could she when they barely knew each other?

Was he just using her?

All her cousins' voices in her head had frightened her, as had the intensity of her emotions, and she'd pulled back.

She didn't want to be just another notch on Pieter's bedpost. Another one of the women he'd dated.

It would be better if they both went their separate ways today. She knew that.

But she couldn't forget hint of vulnerability he'd shown when he'd persuaded her to stay in his room last night. There had been something behind his eyes, something he wasn't saying that had prompted his actions. It confused her.

She ran through the shower and donned the pale jeans and shirt she'd wear for the horsemanship round midmorning. Tonight would be the fashion show, and she wasn't ready to think about that. To remember Pieter as he'd applied her makeup. Close enough to kiss.

When she emerged from the bathroom, Pieter still hadn't returned, but a local newspaper had been shoved beneath the hotel room door. She carried it to the bed and started reading, her ear half on the door to listen for Pieter's arrival.

The current event headlines were depressing, and she flipped to the local news section, where a picture of a beautiful blonde woman in a fancy ballgown graced the front page of the section.

Princess Alessandra of Glorvaird rumored to be in Austin for rodeo.

A real-life princess? Here in town? It seemed ludicrous. McKenna read through the article quickly. It talked about an assassination attempt from months ago, how the princess had met a real Texas cowboy and fallen in love.

There weren't any details about whether the princess would visit the rodeo, only speculation as to why she'd come to Austin and whether the rodeo was the draw.

But niggling questions darted through McKenna's head like minnows in a shallow pond. She didn't know where Glorvaird was—somewhere in Europe, possibly?—but Pieter had an accent. He'd claimed to be attending the rodeo to meet his cousin, but he hadn't said that the meeting was *planned*. His new clothes, the fancy rented truck. How his hands were more manicured than hers.

It was all circumstantial evidence, but… could Pieter be cousin to a princess?

Would that make him a *prince*?

It seemed crazy. Completely crazy.

She heard the electronic lock click as the door unlocked. Pieter pushed the door open slowly, peeking inside.

"Good, you're up." He came into the room and closed the door behind him. He wore a crisp black T-shirt, another pair of pressed, brand-new Wranglers, and those stupid dress boots.

Was he trying to fool someone? Pretending to be

something he wasn't?

It was subtle, but he seemed different than he had yesterday. More closed off. Or maybe she was imagining things, trying to make him fit the image of a prince that was now burned into her brain.

She held up the paper for him to see the princess's photo.

"Is this your cousin? The one you're trying to meet?"

His face went white beneath his tan, which was confirmation—sort of.

She jumped to her feet, unable to remain still. "You're a... a prince? Why didn't you want me to know?"

Why was he trying to dress like a cowboy instead of the royalty he was? That behavior—it was suspicious, that's what it was.

He pushed one hand through his hair. "It's complicated."

She let her hands rest on her hips. "I'll bet. And the country girl wouldn't be able to understand it?"

He frowned. "Ha. Look, I didn't want to announce my arrival because I'm not sure she'll see me if she knows I'm here. We're not...close."

His expression might be closed off, but she sensed he wasn't telling the full truth. "So you didn't tell me because...?"

"What does it matter? I didn't tell anyone. It was a lucky guess on your part."

She snorted. "Not likely, not the way you're trying to dress. And your accent gives you away."

He didn't seem to have a response for that. He twisted a ring on his little finger.

"What's so important about you meeting up with her anyway?"

Pieter turned away. He ran one finger over the edge of the dresser across the room, his shoulders tense and set.

There was a small wall-mounted mirror, and she could see the side of his face, the muscle jumping in his jaw again, and the angry set of his lips.

And she couldn't help remembering what she'd just read. Someone had tried to assassinate the princess.

And suddenly her heart was pounding.

"You're not going to...hurt her. Are you?"

She wasn't sure where she got the courage to say the words. Maybe all those arguments with her cousins, trying to prove she could be something they said she never could.

He didn't respond.

Was his silence confirmation?

After the way he'd insisted she not be alone last night, the things he'd done to help her get here to Austin and get through her first interview, she couldn't imagine him trying to physically harm another person.

Had she been that wrong about him this whole time? *Had* she accepted a ride from a criminal?

She took two sidesteps toward the door.

He caught sight of her in the mirror, whirled, his eyes a little wild. "Are you kidding me? You're scared of me *now*? Not of spending the night in the same room with me, but you think I'll what…try to kill you?"

He was angry. Sparks flew from his eyes, but he didn't make a move toward her. And if she wasn't mistaken, there was also a hint of pain there…

She crossed her arms, stuck out her chin, and stood her ground.

"Then what? Tell me what you came to Austin for. Because sneaking around the way you are doesn't exactly seem like the behavior of someone trying to reconcile a broken relationship."

* * *

Pieter blew out a frustrated breath.

It didn't help.

He'd judged McKenna all wrong. She might be young, and naive, and innocent.

But she wasn't stupid.

She'd figured out his identity from a newspaper article.

"I don't want to *physically* hurt her," he said finally. He felt slimy just admitting this aloud.

Admitting the truth aloud made his plan sound…petty.

"But if I find something that would make her life a little more miserable, I would use it."

It was the least the princess deserved for his pain.

But McKenna looked at him as if she wanted to recoil. As if he'd betrayed *her* somehow.

Which was crazy. He'd saved her from the side of the road yesterday, had provided her food and a safe place to stay. He'd helped her.

He didn't owe her anything.

And he didn't like how he felt when she looked at him like that.

It was a look he'd seen in the mirror, directed at his mother. But he wasn't his mother, and he never would be.

"That's not very...noble," she said finally. Quietly. Like she was resigned that he wasn't going to change his mind.

Why should he?

"I'm afraid my title is more of a formality than anything," he said. He couldn't contain the trace of bitterness in his voice. "My mother was forcibly removed from the kingdom before I was born. I've never met my cousins, never stepped foot in the royal palace. So if I don't act exactly like a prince, perhaps that's why."

Her eyes were shadowed as she looked at him. His words hadn't changed anything. He'd known they wouldn't.

And he couldn't forget the decision he'd come to in the night. It was better to part ways now.

"I'll drive you back to the fairgrounds," he said. "If you want a ride. Or I can call a taxi for you. I've been to the bank and made a withdrawal. I thought...I want you to have it."

He held out the wad of large bills he'd pulled out of the bank earlier. She stared at it as if it was something disgusting.

"I don't want or need your money," she said. "I appreciate all your help, but I can take care of myself."

He'd thought she might say something like that. He shrugged and stuffed the bills in his front pocket—for now. He'd sneak the money into her duffel when he got the chance. Then he'd probably not see her again all weekend.

It was for the best. They both knew it.

But the silence as he drove her back to the fairgrounds was fraught with condemnation, and a boulder that felt suspiciously like guilt settled deep in his gut.

CHAPTER SEVEN

At the rodeo grounds later that morning, Pieter didn't think he was doing a horrible job of blending in with the other cowboys, especially since he'd taken McKenna's advice and worn a plain T-shirt instead of the dressy shirt he'd bought.

He couldn't do anything about the boots now.

Rough-and-tumble men were everywhere, traipsing around the dusty outdoor pens near the rodeo arena. A sense of anticipation swelled in the air, or perhaps it was the pressure and humidity building for the coming storm front predicted to arrive later in the day. Whatever the cause, everyone was talkative, especially the bull riders.

Biking as a sport had its inherent risks—such as getting in a crash at nearly forty miles per hour with nothing but a jersey to protect you from the road—but these guys willingly went into the arena against thousand-pound animals that wanted to kill them.

They were crazy.

Of particular note was a handsome blond bloke who didn't seem to talk or brag all that much. Cody Austin. Pieter had heard it rumored that he and

Gideon Hale, Alessandra's fiancé, were buddies from elementary school or some such. Pieter kept the man in his peripheral vision but hadn't spoken to him.

Instead, Pieter was talking to two other riders not too far from where Austin sat on the pen railing. That's when he caught the perfect opportunity.

Alessandra's fiancé approached Austin. They exchanged a friendly handshake, and Hale asked whether Austin was still coming to his wedding.

It was rumored that the fiancé was special ops, and Pieter could readily believe it the way the man scanned for danger all around him. He had a stance that said he could kill you easily—probably with his little finger.

Hale's eyes skimmed right over Pieter without taking notice. Lucky for him, the two cowboys he was talking to made him look like he belonged.

Pieter talked with the two men long enough for it not to be suspicious and then pretended to take a call on his cell. He edged closer to Austin and Hale.

With his phone to his ear and his arm partially blocking his face, he hoped they wouldn't be able to see that he was eavesdropping.

"…how well do you know Cindy? Rumor is you dated her."

Austin snorted. "You know how the rumor mill can be, especially on the circuit. We've crossed paths a few times, but that's all."

Hale didn't seem about to hear that. "I hoped you might have her number."

"Stepping out on your princess already?" Austin

teased. Brave soul.

That was juicy, but Pieter didn't believe it for a second. Hale was after something else. The question was, what?

One of the bulls in the pen bellowed and butted the fence on the opposite side, snorting and blowing with strings of saliva running down from his mouth.

Hale and Austin were distracted, started talking about bulls and Austin's draw.

Pieter knew he couldn't keep standing here for long without drawing suspicion, so he pretended to hang up the phone and acted as if he were texting instead. His chance to find out anything was dwindling, and he knew it.

And then he got incredibly lucky.

From his peripheral vision, Pieter saw Hale craning his neck to look all around. He spoke in a low voice. "Look, the truth is... Alessandra and I are trying to track down someone, and we think Cindy might be her."

Austin was quiet for a moment. "What, does she owe you money?"

Hale sized up his friend. "You seem awfully protective for someone who's only an acquaintance."

Austin gave a one-shouldered shrug. "Folks on the circuit gotta look out for each other." Nice evasion.

Hale was silent for a long moment, focusing on the other man. Finally, he sighed. When he spoke, his voice was even lower, and Pieter had to strain to hear.

"Alessandra's... half-sister...just found out...trying

to locate her..."

A half-sister? Now *that* was the kind of information Pieter had hoped to find. He'd read every biography, newspaper article, and tabloid story about his cousins and the King. Once, he'd even attempted to bribe a royal staffer. There'd never been any hint of a scandal of this proportion.

An illegitimate child. A lost princess.

He turned away, satisfied for now that he had something he could use against the royal family when the timing was right. He definitely didn't want to draw Hale's attention. He ducked behind a stock trailer, pausing for a moment just to digest this new information.

Leaking this to the press would put a dark spot on the royal family's reputations and would likely create a media storm.

And... It sounded as if Alessandra wanted to find her sister. If a media storm blew up, would the sister she didn't know pull back from the relationship?

Now *that* was a punishment fitting for his cousins. But... Was it enough?

He needed to think about this.

He was making his way among the trucks and trailers when he caught a flash of what might be McKenna's hair.

She had her riding event this morning, didn't she?

He shouldn't go anywhere near her. She knew his identity and if she wanted to, could blow any sense of cover he had. Although now that he had this information about a lost princess, he wasn't sure he needed to keep his identity hidden.

And somehow he couldn't keep his feet from taking him in that direction.

He didn't have to talk to her. Didn't have to get close to her. He'd stand in the back somewhere and watch.

Just watch.

* * *

McKenna waited on Maximus's back, just outside the arena gate. Another few seconds and she'd be riding the horsemanship pattern in front of judges, contestants and a smattering of onlookers.

Don't blow it.

She and the other contestants had received notes on the horsemanship pattern, which was identical for all riders. If she couldn't remember the pattern and direct Maximus around the outdoor arena, she would lose points. If she couldn't get Maximus to obey, she'd lose points. If she was unseated, she could kiss her chances for winning goodbye.

And then, after the first round, she'd have to repeat the pattern on one of her competitors' horses. That might be the worst part, depending on how difficult or cranky an unknown horse could be. And it was luck of the draw.

"We can do this," she whispered to Maximus from her seat in the saddle. The other contestant exited the arena and McKenna nudged her horse forward.

She tried to ignore the judges, who were sitting on

the front row of the arena stands. Ignored the building thunderheads above that made it necessary for the arena lights to be switched on.

Just concentrate on the pattern.

She raced Max across the dirt-packed arena floor and drew him up short, almost sending him to his haunches.

She nearly slipped her seat on the saddle and had to clamp her thighs tightly around Max to keep from doing so.

She hadn't meant to do *that*.

Face flaming at the amateur mistake, she forced a long exhale through her lips and kept moving. Left turn. Sidestep. Backwards. Tight circle.

Almost there.

She'd barely blinked and then was guiding Maximus out of the arena to a smattering of applause. She released the breath she'd been holding.

She maneuvered Max out of the way of the gates, where the next queen contestant, a young woman wearing bright pink from her hat to her boots, waited to be called inside. McKenna slipped off the horse.

She leaned her face against Max's shoulder. Maybe hiding a little. Distant thunder rolled, and Max's skin flickered, a sign of nerves.

"Good job," a female voice said from nearby.

McKenna looked across Max's back to see a girl in a pair of blue jeans, a purple dress shirt, and a white hat. She realized this girl had gone two ahead of her.

"I could've done better," McKenna said. "But thanks."

The girl winked. "I think that same thing every time I come out of the ring. I'm Danielle."

"McKenna."

"You're better than ninety percent of the other girls," Danielle said. "The rest is how the judges score it. Everyone makes little mistakes. Don't sweat it."

This girl thought McKenna was better than most of the other competitors? Was she for real?

Danielle must've seen the disbelief on McKenna's features because she laughed, a soft trilling sound that had Max's ears flicking, though he remained alert and calm.

"Is this your first contest?" Danielle asked.

"I won my hometown title last summer," McKenna said. "But I'm a total newbie."

"Well, you're a natural. Some of us have been going it awhile, and we don't handle our horses like you just did."

McKenna's face heated again at the unexpected praise. "How many times have you competed?"

"Too many to count. My mom and older sister made it all the way to Miss Rodeo USA, and I've been queening since I was eight."

Wow.

Danielle laughed again, softer this time and a little bitterly. "Yeah. It's a lot of pressure. If I can't get there this year, I'm out."

But at least she had family supporting her. Helping her.

McKenna was all alone, and too conscious of the fact since Pieter and she had parted ways earlier in the day.

"So your beau is a total hunk," Danielle said, breaking McKenna out of her morose thoughts.

"What?" she half-laughed. "I don't have a—"

Danielle pointed to the stands, and McKenna could see Pieter sitting at the highest level, not quite hidden in shadow but obviously trying not to be noticed.

As if someone like him could hide in plain sight. The man commanded attention wherever he went. Like yesterday in the diner, and just this morning he'd turned heads as they'd walked through the hotel lobby.

She couldn't see from this distance, but now that Danielle had pointed him out, McKenna felt Pieter's piercing gaze on her.

"He's been staring at you since before your ride," Danielle said.

"He's not my beau." McKenna averted her eyes.

Maybe she shouldn't have said what she'd said at the hotel, but she'd been blindsided to see another side of the man she'd come to think of as a hero. Which was silly, because she'd barely known him thirty-six hours.

Before she could protest again, the head judge moved to the side of the stands with a piece of paper in hand.

"She's posting the draw for the next round," Danielle said.

McKenna couldn't think about Pieter. All she had left was her dream. She couldn't afford to mess it up now.

* * *

There was an announcement—a break due to the severe weather gathering overhead. Sprinkles splattered the metal bleachers even as the voice said they'd reconvene mid-morning tomorrow. The stands around the arena quickly emptied.

Pieter's stomach was gurgling, and he figured he'd tortured himself enough watching McKenna. She rode like a queen, controlling her horse with expert movements and exquisite grace.

She wasn't like anyone he'd ever met before.

Why did she have to appeal to him so very much? He'd dated plenty of women, wealthy, polished women, but there was something about her...

He made his way through the small throng of people huddling beneath a batch of umbrellas, careful to watch ahead and make sure he wasn't going to bump into McKenna.

But once he'd navigated around the largest cluster of people, loud voices drew his attention. There was a scuffle near the trailer lot. And he couldn't help but focus in on the black horse and the woman in the tan hat who seemed to be at the center.

He knew trouble when he saw it, and just the fact that McKenna was in the midst of it had him pushing past a few slow-moving grandmas.

Two men who could pass for taller versions of McKenna with their brown hair and hazel eyes flanked her, one attempting to edge between her and her horse.

"You've humiliated yourself enough."

"And us."

McKenna shook her head. Even from several yards away—and closing—he could see the color rising in her face. "How exactly have I humiliated you?"

"Everybody back home is talking—"

"That's their problem. Not mine."

Good girl.

Pieter was aware of the curious glances from several of the people nearby. And…was that one of the judges standing at a slight distance, watching?

The cousin closest to Pieter reached out and grabbed her elbow. "Look, you had your fun. It's time to go home."

McKenna tried to shake him off, but he was a head taller than she was, obviously much stronger, and he didn't let go.

Her horse neighed and bobbed its head, agitated. Thunder clapped loudly, and the horse's eyes went a little wild, the whites showing.

The girl standing a few feet from Pieter's elbow, the one he'd seen chatting with McKenna outside the ring, looked over at him. "If the judges see this, McKenna might be disqualified for poor behavior."

He didn't know why this girl thought *he* had anything to do with the situation, but her words were like taking a spill off his bike. He knew how much this event meant to McKenna.

He jogged a couple of steps and put himself between McKenna and her cousin, forcing the man to drop his hold on her.

He stepped closer, got into Pieter's face. "Who're you?"

"Todd…" McKenna said.

So this was the cousin who'd belittled her on the phone.

"If you want to talk, let's find somewhere more private," Pieter said, using the same commanding tone he'd affected with his mother when she wasn't in a mood to be reasoned with. "Or better yet, let's meet up after McKenna's next ride tomorrow. She needs to concentrate."

"She needs to come home," the second cousin said, joining his brother in Pieter's space.

Pieter glanced to see that the judge had remained where she was, and her entire focus was on this confrontation.

She could be disqualified.

He looked at McKenna, who stood at his elbow, and saw the resignation in her eyes. She was fully expecting her cousins to ruin her chances at being crowned rodeo queen.

He wasn't so accepting.

He smiled at her. "Why don't you take Maximus to his stall, and we'll meet up near your trailer," he suggested. The storms were threatening, but at least they could have a modicum of privacy there, in case her cousins got loud. He suspected they might.

Miraculously, her cousins agreed.

He waited until McKenna had led the horse away, then followed the cousins to the parking lot to make sure they didn't make more trouble for her. The two brothers stood several feet from him, arms crossed and silent. Tension roiled as thick as the humid pre-storm air.

McKenna joined them minutes later, panting and out of breath.

She slanted a glance at him. He couldn't tell whether she was relieved he was still here or wanted him to leave.

"Who's this guy, Kenna?" not-Todd asked, jerking his thumb in Pieter's direction.

Lightning flashed in the distance. The air around them felt electric with the storm about to break.

"A friend," he said

Todd laughed. "Oh, that's rich. Some rich boy like you making friends with our cousin?"

McKenna's face went crimson.

"This the guy who drove you down here?" not-Todd asked.

McKenna nodded.

"How much did you put out to get him to help you? You little—"

"That's enough," Pieter said, hearing the dangerous tone to his voice. He felt on the verge of losing control, his hands shaking as he fought to hold onto it. He couldn't lose his temper like his mother. "You shouldn't speak of McKenna like that."

Not-Todd's eyebrows went up. He took a step into Pieter's personal space but looked at McKenna.

"Awful protective for someone you're not sleeping with."

"You should be more respectful of your own flesh and blood." His voice was cold, angry. He didn't back down, though the man had at least an inch and twenty pounds on him. And there were two of them.

"You should mind your own business," not-Todd said. "We've been telling her for years to watch who she sells her body to—"

Before he'd meant to move, he'd thrown the punch. The other man didn't see it coming.

Not-Todd went down, hard, but that left Pieter open to Todd's attack.

* * *

"I can't believe you did that," McKenna murmured.

She knelt in front of the trailer where Pieter sat holding a paper napkin to his lower lip.

His bleeding lower lip.

"They shouldn't disrespect you like that," he mumbled, but he wasn't quite meeting her eye.

She put both hands on his thighs, and his head came up, though he still held the napkin to his lip.

"No one's ever done something like that for me before," she said softly.

She hadn't believed it when she'd seen Pieter throw the first punch, had stood in shock when Todd responded with one of his own. She thanked God a security guard had arrived—said he'd heard from a gal named Danielle that there might be trouble out here. He'd broken up the fight and told her cousins the police would be called if they didn't get lost.

Her cousins had been escorted from the property and ordered not to come back. Which was a relief, but also had her second guessing herself. Was she doing all of this—and alienating the only family she had left—for nothing? Was it going to be worth it in the end?

She brushed a few strands of her hair out of her eyes. The humidity from the building storm was ruining her carefully-crafted curls. She looked down at the gravel between their knees.

"Maybe they're right," she said softly. "Maybe I *should* go home. I'm not sure I belong here. The other girls…"

"Your aunt and uncle should've taught them better," he said hotly. "They should be supporting you, not belittling you."

Her lips formed a sad smile. "My aunt and uncle might've taken me in, but they never bothered to care."

Pieter touched her chin, tipped her face up. "I know a little something about unfit parents."

"Your mom?" she guessed.

He nodded tightly. "Bi-polar. *And* schizophrenic." He snorted softly. "As if one weren't bad enough. Father's never been in the picture and…"

"I'm sorry." Her cousins weren't the easiest to live with, but his childhood sounded even worse than hers had been.

He clasped her hand and held it loosely between them. "You've worked hard to get here. You can't give up now."

She wrinkled her nose, made a face. "What if it was a fluke—the other contest?"

"It wasn't."

Looking into his confident, clear gaze, she could almost believe him. Wanted to, so very badly.

"You'll hate yourself if you give up now—if you don't even try."

He was right.

"I was a little surprised to see you watching the horsemanship contest," she said. "And you've come to my rescue again."

A hint of color crept into his neck, the only visible reaction to her words.

And so she went for it all. "You're more than this desire for revenge you carry," she whispered. "More than whatever it is your family's done to you." With a schizophrenic mother, she couldn't imagine what he'd been through.

His eyes were wary and watchful as she reached up. She pulled his hand away from his lip, took the napkin from him. There was only a small touch of blood on it, a small swelling at the corner of his mouth. He'd mostly evaded Todd's hit, even when her cousin had had the element of surprise.

"You've been my prince since this whole thing started," she said, looking straight into his face. "There has to be a better way to confront the situation than whatever you're planning. Act like the prince that you are."

She rose up from her crouch, surprising him as she brushed his lips with hers.

She couldn't maintain the kiss for more than a few seconds, which was fine, because her face was flaming now, and she couldn't help but compare herself to all the women he'd probably kissed before.

She stood straight as another growl of thunder ripped through the sky. "I've got to check on Maximus. And get ready for tomorrow."

She didn't look back as she made her way to the stables.

Because she wasn't giving up yet. Not on being rodeo queen.

And not on the prince she'd begun to care for.

CHAPTER EIGHT

Sequestered in his hotel room later that afternoon, Pieter lay on the bed with his arms folded behind his head and stared at the ceiling again as rain poured down outside.

Turned out the bed wasn't much more comfortable than the floor.

Or maybe it was his own conscience that made it impossible for him to rest.

His mind had been spinning since McKenna had kissed him earlier in the afternoon.

He didn't understand her. How she could be treated so poorly by her family and still be kindhearted. She was driven, but not bitter.

She'd said he could *be better.*

The words had been like a cleansing waterfall, releasing something inside of him.

Or maybe it was her kiss that had felt like absolution. Like forgiveness, which he most certainly didn't deserve.

He didn't have to be like his mother. Seeking revenge, always grieving a crown that wasn't hers to have.

He could take the high road. Keep what he'd learned about the lost princess to himself, though it went against every molecule in his body not to use the information as a bargaining chip to benefit himself.

He could be worthy of McKenna. If he gave up his quest for revenge.

Did he want to do it?

Could he do it?

And if he did, what was he doing here in Austin? He'd come all this way. Could he leave empty-handed?

And what about McKenna? She had plans. Was college bound—he believed she'd get there eventually—and law school meant extra years in the classroom.

Was there even room in her life for him?

He didn't know.

But he wanted to find out.

* * *

It was just after lunch the day after Gideon had met with his friend Cody Austin when the knock came at the door of their suite.

Alessandra glanced nervously at her fiancé as he went to the door. Out of habit, she smoothed the long pencil skirt she wore, standing beside the sofa but not moving.

She didn't want to scare her new sister the moment she walked in the door.

"Relax," Gideon said. He nodded to her hands, which she realized she'd twisted in front of her.

She was so nervous. This was a big moment for her. For her entire family.

She heard the murmur of his voice, but not his exact words as he opened the door.

And then a young woman followed him inside the suite, looking around in wide-eyed wonder. She was only a year or so younger than Alessandra. While Alessandra and her two biological sisters Eloise and Mia shared the same almost platinum blonde hair, Cindy's hair was more dirty blonde and was cut around her shoulders. Her eyes were brown instead of the blue Alessandra had expected.

But there was a different mother in the picture, she reminded herself. Of course her half-sister wouldn't be an identical match for the three princesses.

"Hello," Alessandra said, hoping her voice didn't betray her nerves.

"Howdy." Cindy nodded in Alessandra's direction, though her eyes still flicked around the room, taking everything in. "Nice place you got here."

"Won't you sit down?" Alessandra indicated the sofa facing hers, which would put a coffee table between them. "We've ordered refreshments, if you'd like a glass of tea or water."

The other woman sat, so Alessandra did as well. Gideon perched on the arm of the sofa beside her.

"I'm not that thirsty. Just real curious why I got a mysterious summons to meet you here. You really a princess?"

The girl's diction wasn't the best, and her twangy accent was much worse than Gideon's. But Alessandra could overlook that.

"We have a couple of questions for you," Gideon shot Alessandra a look that she interpreted as *don't jump the gun.*

She appreciated her fiancé and his careful approach, but she just really wanted to know if Cindy was her sister.

"Where were you born?" Gideon asked.

"Lubbock, Texas," the girl responded, though she looked a little suspicious.

"Have you ever lived in Kalispell, Montana?" Gideon asked.

Cindy crossed her arms. "For a little while. Why?"

Gideon put a hand to Alessandra's shoulder. "We're looking for someone. We've been keeping things very private, but Alessandra recently found out she has a half sister."

The other woman suddenly pealed with laughter.

Startled, Alessandra looked at Gideon, who appeared as flummoxed as she felt.

Cindy slapped her thigh and even wiped away tears before she quieted. "And you think"—she hiccoughed—"you think *I'm a princess?*"

Alessandra swallowed the unease that rose in her throat. "Yes."

Gideon shot her another look. "Your birthdate matches," Gideon said. "We'd tried to verify your birth certificate, but we've been running into roadblocks."

Cindy shook her head. "I'm not who you're looking for," she said, now serious.

"Our father—" Alessandra started, but Cindy interrupted.

"I know my dad. He's a deadbeat, not a king. Believe me, as a little girl, I wished all the time for someone to come and take me away."

Alessandra shivered.

Now the other woman stood. "This has been fun." Her tone indicated it had been anything *but*. "I'm sorry I'm not who you're looking for."

Gideon stood too, but Alessandra's legs were shaky and felt too weak to hold her.

"Would you consent to letting us do a DNA test, just to make sure?" Gideon asked quickly. "It's just a swab on the inside of your cheek."

Cindy shrugged. "I guess that'd be fine. Won't do you any good, though."

She and Gideon conversed in low tones as he helped her with the test. Just a few minutes had passed when Gideon stuck what looked like a cotton swab in some kind of plastic tube and then sealed it in an envelope.

Thirty seconds later, Cindy ducked out of the suite.

Alessandra remained on the sofa, stunned and inexplicably hurt.

That had gone all wrong.

* * *

Later that night, Gideon found Alessandra staring out the hotel room window at the Austin skyline. She'd barely touched her dinner, hadn't wanted to talk after Cindy had left the suite earlier.

He hated seeing her despondent. He'd tried to warn her that things might not go smoothly in this search for the lost princess.

Now he sidled up behind her at the window, set his hands on her waist.

Thankfully, she leaned back against him, settling her head in the hollow of his shoulder.

He watched her reflection as she stared out the window. He search for any sign of tears. Alessandra was good at hiding her feelings, though usually not from him.

"I'm sorry things didn't go the way you wanted," he said softly.

She breathed in deeply. "You told me it wouldn't be simple."

"Doesn't mean I didn't want it to be."

She breathed in again, and it was shaky this time. "Thank you for that. Do you think we'll ever find her?"

"It's hard to stay hidden forever, at least from what I've seen. The DNA test might still come back with a different result than she thinks."

He didn't know whether to hope that could be true or not.

He talked Alessandra into sitting beside him on the couch as the room darkened around them. She curled into his side, and they played a local news station.

And then he was reaching for the remote and turning up the volume as a reporter interviewed a dark-haired man outside the rodeo fairgrounds.

He vaguely recognized the man, maybe had passed by him earlier or in the few days he'd been scouting the venue.

Now the man was dressed in a finely tailored suit. He spoke with the same light, cultured accent similar to Alessandra's.

"…name is Prince Pieter of Glorvaird. My mother was estranged from her family before she was born."

Alessandra sat up and perched on the edge of the couch.

"You know this guy?"

She shook her head. "I've never met my cousin."

"I'm seeking reconciliation with the royal family and have some information concerning recent attempts on the princess's lives that may be of interest."

The camera zoomed in on the guy. Dark hair, blue eyes. He looked very little like Alessandra, but the way he carried himself, the high cheekbones.

"I have no ulterior motives and would welcome a meeting with my cousin and whatever security she deems necessary."

The news moved on to other stories, but Alessandra continued to stare at the screen. Then she turned to him, her face curiously blank. "Do you think he meant it? That he wants reconciliation with our family?"

Gideon shrugged. "I'm more interested in what he said about the attempt on your life. You told me in the beginning you thought your aunt was trying to kill you."

She was quiet for a long moment. "Do you think he's a part of it? That he could be trying to make an attempt of his own?"

"I think that'd be pretty stupid after he just went on TV and announced himself." But of course Gideon was suspicious.

"You should call your sister," he said. "Maybe have Eloise talk to your dad. We need to find out why your aunt was banished and what he thinks about meeting with this Pieter guy."

She nodded slowly. He knew she had a tumultuous relationship with her father, but if the king told her not to meet with this cousin, Alessandra likely wouldn't.

But that didn't mean Gideon couldn't meet with him. He wanted answers about the attempt on Alessandra's life and assurance that it wasn't going to happen again.

He'd do anything to protect the woman he loved.

CHAPTER NINE

Pieter had gotten the call late last night, but he hadn't been sleeping, as he'd been waiting for it.

He'd agreed to meet Alessandra's fiancé for breakfast in the hotel restaurant.

The firm knock on his door shouldn't have been a surprise. He finished knotting his tie and looked through the peephole. Gideon Hale.

He should have expected this. Didn't his mother love to show up unexpectedly? It was an intimidation technique Pieter was familiar with.

But today he wouldn't be intimidated. He fixed McKenna's kiss in his mind and opened the door. The former Navy SEAL pushed his way inside—Pieter was no match for his honed strength and didn't even try to block Hale's way.

He endured the pat down the other man insisted on and then straightened his tie and jacket as Hale proceeded to open the closet and every drawer in the room, even ducked into the bare washroom. Pieter stood in the center of the room, watching and waiting.

"If I was planning something against Alessandra,

do you really think I'd leave evidence in my hotel room?"

He knew it was the wrong thing to say but resented the other man's suspicion. It wasn't as if the assassination attempt had been *his* idea.

"*Are* you planning something against Alessandra?" Hale got in his face. "Because I'll do anything to protect her."

It was a real threat, one that Pieter met head-on. He spoke steadily. "The only thing I want from my cousin is to reconnect with her. Our families have been separated long enough."

Hale continued his stare down, and Pieter met his gaze evenly. For once, he had nothing to hide. It was a feeling he'd rarely experienced.

Finally, Hale stepped back with a slow nod. "She said the same thing."

Pieter experienced a moment of hope. Maybe she was downstairs, waiting in the restaurant, but it was quickly extinguished when Hale said, "She's in talks with her sister and the king."

Whatever hope he'd been feeling disintegrated. The king had been the one to send his mother away, the one to keep both of them away.

"I think you'll find things have changed a lot in Glorvaird," Hale said, still slightly wary. "The king is...not well."

Pieter experienced a pang of sympathy for his cousin, one that would've been foreign to him before McKenna.

"Tell me what happened in New York," Hale

demanded.

"Can we at least get breakfast? I'm starving." And ready to be in public instead of this private room with this very large, aggressive man.

Hale agreed grudgingly.

The restaurant in the hotel lobby was bustling with patrons.

As Hale sat across from Pieter, a flash went off from a few yards away.

A hostess rushed over to escort the camera-toting reporter out of the restaurant.

Hale glared at Pieter, who shrugged and smiled a little fiercely. He might be changing his stripes, but that didn't mean he had to give over *every* advantage. If the press saw him with Alessandra's fiancé, they would report favorably about him.

A waitress took their orders and filled their mugs with coffee. The booth in the corner was semi-private, and when she left, Gideon leaned forward. "Start talking."

Pieter told the solider about going on tour with the cyclists and returning home to discover his mother's sinister plot, how she'd gone off her meds and hired an assassin. He also shared what he'd done to fix it, paying off the men his mother had hired and heightening security around her.

He went on to explain how he'd come here to enact revenge on the royal family and even the fact that he'd gotten close enough to discover their secret mission. "But I won't do anything with the information."

Gideon looked skeptical. "Why the change of heart?"

Pieter's gaze was drawn behind his companion to a slender figure standing in the entryway near the hostess stand. McKenna.

What was she doing here? He hadn't seen her since last night.

Gideon turned, following Pieter's gaze.

Pieter half stood, letting McKenna catch sight of him and then enduring Gideon's curious look as he stood to greet her.

She wore a pair of what must be favorite jeans, worn as they were, and a tank top. Her hair was pulled in a ponytail behind her head. She looked just as she was, young and fresh and wholesome.

And she made his heart pound.

"Hey." She bussed his cheek with a kiss.

He was surprised by the confident move and found his hand rested at her waist naturally.

"You look... Princely." She looked him up and down, taking in the suit and tie, his usual apparel. He wasn't sorry to say goodbye to the cowboy-imposter clothes.

She looked delectable. If they were alone, he'd kiss her properly, find out why she'd sought him out this morning. He was brimming with hope.

But he was uncomfortably aware of Hale's gaze on his back. And then the other man said, "Why don't you join us...?"

There was nothing to do but make introductions.

McKenna slipped into the booth where he'd just

vacated his seat, leaving him to slide in beside her.

The waitress brought their food, and McKenna declined to order anything, saying she'd eaten with a friend earlier.

He snuck her a piece of bacon anyway and grinned a little when she sipped from his coffee mug.

But his grin faded when Hale said, "I'd like to hear more about your mother."

* * *

McKenna felt the tension overtake Pieter and couldn't help reaching for him. She'd spent the night with Danielle and her mother in their RV, and they'd all been watching the evening news when she'd seen Pieter's segment.

She was running on instinct, coming to his hotel this morning. She'd only hoped to see him, talk to him after seeing him on TV.

She'd told him he could act the prince, and he had.

And maybe a small part of her wanted to know whether he was still enacting his plan for revenge or if he was genuine in his desire for reconciliation with his family.

And now Gideon Hale had asked the hardest question of all. Pieter had mentioned his mother's mental illness but not gone into detail.

If he was really changed, if he was moving forward with his life trying to live up to the title nobody seemed to think he deserved, wouldn't he tell Mr. Hale what he wanted to know?

"One of my earliest memories is of my mother going into one of her rages," Pieter said quietly. He set his fork aside. Maybe talking about his mother made his appetite disappear.

She sidled closer on the bench and curled her fingers around the fist in his lap.

"Sometimes hours later, maybe the next day, she'd be apologetic and tearful, begging forgiveness."

He paused, and she saw the bob of his Adams' apple as he swallowed.

"With Mother, it's often impossible to tell whether she's genuine or trying to manipulate. Sometimes her tearful apologies were real, and others, they were simply designed to win me into her good graces once again."

How awful. She'd often longed for the mother she'd never known, but this... To know that your own mother was manipulating you... She couldn't fathom it.

"When I was a teenager, I tried to hide Mother's condition from everyone. I was embarrassed, ashamed. And there was always that part of me that ached for mother's approval—"

He broke off, continued with, "That's neither here nor there."

As if his feelings didn't matter.

"When the press began printing stories about her decline, she would—well, if she saw the newspaper, she would go into a rage. I was able to nudge her out of the public eye and have spent a lot of money hiring caretakers and doctors that would keep quiet."

Gideon nodded solemnly.

"I tell you this so you understand that my mother is not well and that her motives are not always clear. She often disappears in her own head for weeks at a time."

His shoulders steadied. "I don't know what happened between my mother and the king, only that she speaks sometimes of betrayal and plots. Whatever passed between her and your future father-in-law happened before I was born, before Alessandra was born. Whether my mother can be welcomed back into the royal circle, I don't know, but I shouldn't be exiled for something I had no part of."

Gideon sipped his coffee before speaking. "I can't guarantee a meeting," he said. "Alessandra is very careful with fulfilling her family duties. If Eloise or the King decline a meeting, I don't know that she'll go against them."

Pieter's hand tightened in its fist , though he betrayed no other outward sign of emotion. "I understand."

"But…" She started to say something. She didn't know what, but Pieter had come so far, and Gideon couldn't even see it...

Gideon nodded at her, then returned his gaze to Pieter. "Alessandra is very interested in reconnecting the family. I think with her father's condition uncertain and not knowing how much time he might have left, it's been hard on her. I think she's more aware how important family connections are."

Some of Pieter's awful tension eased at that. Enough that he released his fist and threaded their fingers together beneath the table.

It wasn't assurance that he'd get to meet his cousin, but it was a sign, however small, that his cousin hadn't rejected him.

* * *

Alessandra paced the unfamiliar suite's living area. She was unaccountably nervous.

What was Pieter like? Would he like her?

After Gideon's rendezvous with Pieter, she and her fiancé had made a video call to speak with her father and Eloise. They'd given tentative approval for a meeting.

And now the meeting time was here.

She'd also spoken to Mia on the phone earlier, and her sister had been just as excited about the meeting as Alessandra and wanted a full report as soon as he left.

Pieter was dark where she was light—Gideon had managed to find a picture of her cousin—and the wariness in his gaze as he entered the small sitting room at a separate hotel from where she and Gideon were staying threatened her composure. Gideon was taking no chances with her safety, even though he believed Pieter's intentions to be good.

"Thank you for taking the meeting with me," her cousin said, reaching forward, probably to give her hand a royal kiss, but she stepped toward him with both arms out.

He accepted her hug, embracing her loosely as Gideon watched.

Pieter's distance, the wary way he held himself, brought tears, and she found herself sniffling as they stepped apart.

"I'm sorry," she said, wiping away the few tears that fell.

Pieter looked as if he had no idea what to do with her tears. His eyes were wide, almost panicked.

Gideon chuckled and motioned the other man to sit down. Pieter took a wingback chair, leaving her and Gideon the sofa.

"I've been curious about you for a long time," she said. "I wanted to know you."

Pieter's expression was shuttered, but she had to believe she saw something like relief pass through his dark eyes.

"I've long wondered about you as well."

Gideon's phone buzzed from his hip pocket, and he excused himself to take the call. She didn't miss the tense lines around his face. She watched Gideon pace back and forth in front of the window on the opposite side of the room. His voice was low, and she couldn't hear what he was saying, but his expression grew more and more concerned.

She forced herself to concentrate on her cousin. "Gideon tells me you've someone special."

He lit up from within, though he remained reserved. It reminded her of her own expression in the mirror when she thought about Gideon and how much she loved him.

"It's very new—" Pieter started.

"We've got a problem," Gideon thundered, rushing back across the room. He reached for Alessandra, and she found herself being pulled to her feet before she even knew what was happening.

Gideon leveled a pointed finger on Pieter. "Your mother is missing. She's escaped the mental institution, and the orderly who helped her says she's bent on destroying the royal family."

Pieter looked as stunned as she felt. "I spoke to her last week. How could she have just left?"

Gideon squeezed Alessandra's elbow. "Perhaps you should've taken more precautions before *you* left the country."

She wanted to shush him, to keep him from wrecking the budding relationship with her cousin with his suspicions and protective nature, but he was already pulling her from the room. She knew he'd be on high alert, and she'd be in lockdown mode until he could pull in enough security to feel a modicum of safety again.

Why this? Why now?

CHAPTER TEN

McKenna stood "backstage" just before the fashion event of the pageant was about to begin, trying to calm her racing heart.

Each contestant would be called on stage, where she'd have to model her own fashion statement in western wear. The host judge would ask one question, drawn randomly from a pool of questions, and the contestant would have to answer in front of all these people. Then the contestants would line up on the long stage.

They had to wait, in front of everyone, as final scores were tabulated.

And then the new queen would be announced.

This was it.

Everything she'd worked for depended on this event. Although the scores for the horsemanship rounds and private interviews weren't publicized, she knew that without a good score in the fashion round, it would be impossible to win.

She was thankful her cousins hadn't shown back up, though she wondered if they'd returned home or were still waiting to watch her fail.

A cool hand touched her forearm, and she turned to fine Danielle at her elbow.

"I'm so nervous," the young woman whispered.

"But you've done this hundreds of times."

"Doesn't mean it gets any easier to walk out there and be judged on your appearance."

They shared a knowing look.

When the second round of the horsemanship competition had resumed yesterday, Danielle had found her. She'd thought maybe the young woman was looking for gossip, wanting to know what had happened with McKenna's cousins, but she'd been utterly surprised when Danielle had checked to see if she was all right.

Like a friend might.

When Danielle had found out McKenna didn't have any place to stay, she had offered a second bunk in her travel trailer, and McKenna had accepted, knowing she couldn't displace Pieter from his bed again.

Plus, after the kiss she'd delivered to him, she didn't know how to classify their relationship.

She'd been proud to be beside him at breakfast, but she'd had to leave to check on Maximus at the arena. She'd heard too many horror stories of horses injuring themselves because of being in unfamiliar surroundings. She wasn't about to leave him for long.

She didn't know whether she and Pieter could move forward from here. He was a prince. He was reconciling with his royal cousins.

And she had her own mission. First university,

then law school.

"He's here," Danielle said, as if she knew who was on McKenna's mind. "About halfway up the stands, left side of the aisle."

McKenna peeked through a crack in the heavy curtain and caught sight of Pieter.

He'd come to see the final event. Because he cared for her, or just to see it through?

She didn't know, and there wasn't time to dwell on it, because the rest of the contestants were lining up behind the curtain. It was time to strut her stuff.

She had no strut, and she barely had any stuff.

But she wore the best charming smile she could muster as she walked onstage.

* * *

"First runner up… McKenna Hastings!"

First runner up.

It wasn't what she wanted, but it was something.

Pieter watched as she graciously hugged the winning rodeo queen. Her smile seemed genuine.

Would she be disappointed? Excited? She'd beat out thirty other women, so she should be pleased. He waited in the stands as the other competitors and their families dispersed and the arena began to clear out.

He watched her talking to the young woman who'd called security the day before. They seemed to be friends now, and he knew that McKenna needed one.

Now the question remained...did McKenna need *him*? Did she have room in her life for a reformed prince?

He hung back near the bottom of the stands, and then finally she walked toward him. Her makeup was impeccable. The western-style long denim skirt with all its sparkles and a simple snap shirt accentuated her trim shape.

Her face was alight, though he read the slight disappointment beneath.

"Congratulations," he said, reaching out to take both of her hands in his.

She let him, which was one relief.

"I know it isn't what you wanted, but this could be a start for you."

She smiled, and her lips trembled a little. "Danielle...well, she made me an offer. She said I could travel along with her and her mom, bunk with them. They're hitting nearly every big pageant this season."

His insides squeezed hard. So she could still chase her dream.

He twisted his family crest ring. "That's wonderful."

Her brows crinkled. "What's the matter?"

"I have to visit Glorvaird." It was the last thing he wanted to say.

Her countenance fell. "Oh."

"It's my mother. She's disappeared."

McKenna's eyes widened. "Oh no."

"Oh yes," he said. "From what I can gather, she

coerced one of the orderlies to help her, and she just walked out of the institution. I've tried calling her, phoning some of her local friends"—not that there were many—"but she's simply vanished."

"I bet your cousin wasn't happy."

"No." But it hadn't been Alessandra's reaction that bothered him. Gideon was the one he'd been slightly afraid of. After the soldier had told him the news, they'd descended into a shouting match until Alessandra had calmed her husband.

Gideon couldn't possibly blame him any more than Pieter blamed himself. He'd missed calls from the institution, telling him of Mother's escape. If he'd checked his messages sooner, would he have been able to rush home and find her before she'd completely disappeared?

There was a part of him that wanted to let it all go. Why did he have to be responsible for Mother? Wasn't she an adult, responsible for herself? He was so weary of it... Hadn't he suffered long enough? Of course, he knew she wasn't sane. Couldn't be expected to watch over herself.

McKenna seemed to understand his conflicting emotions. Her eyes were soft and compassionate.

Then her lips trembled slightly. "I'll pray for you to find her quickly. And for your peace."

He hated this. "I wish..." He swallowed against the hot knot in his throat that wanted to choke him.

She squeezed his hand, and he couldn't face the innocence in her eyes.

He looked down. "I wish things were different."

That *he* was different.

The hall had slowly emptied around them. It was silent now, enough so he heard her soft sigh. "We both know we have to play the hand we're dealt."

He screwed up all his courage and met her eyes. "I'd like to..." Darn, this was hard. "We've only known each other a couple of days, but I think it's safe to say I'm falling in love with you."

Soft color crept into her face. "Me too."

Relief smacked him in the solar plexus and made it hard to breathe. He maneuvered her into a loose embrace, leaning his forehead to hers.

"I should probably try to talk you out of your feelings," he said, "but I'm too selfish for that." He breathed in deeply, trying to memorize her scent. "You've got a bright future—big things ahead. I don't want to take any of that from you. And I've still got to travel to Glovaird. But I'd really like it if you'd wear my ring. As a...promise."

She inhaled sharply as he let go of her to pry the gold ring from his finger. His hands were trembling. He knew he didn't deserve her, but by some miracle, she seemed to want him.

She allowed him to slip the ring on her fourth finger, and he curled her hand in his to admire his family's crest against her skin.

He lifted her hand to kiss her knuckles. "Until I can replace it with another kind of ring."

Her lashes were clumped with tears as she smiled up at him. He was happy—the happiest he'd ever been in his life—and found himself smiling like an idiot.

"Isn't this the part where you kiss me?" she asked.

"I'm trying not to mess anything up," he returned. He would work harder than he ever had, make whatever sacrifices he had to make, if it meant keeping McKenna for his own.

Her hands curled around his neck, and her fingers threaded into the hair at his nape. "Then I *definitely* think you'd better kiss me."

So he did.

EPILOGUE

Three weeks after Alessandra's return to Glorvaird, Crown Princess Eloise sat in the family parlor in the centuries-old castle, listening to her two younger sisters argue. The DNA test for the barrel racer named Cindy had come up negative, leaving them without a lead as to their missing half sister.

But what the two sisters argued about now was of much less importance.

"Lilies are prettier," Mia said.

"But roses are classic," Alessandra returned.

Eloise's future brother-in-law, Gideon, walked in to the room, pocketing his cell phone and frowning fiercely. He'd been particularly intense since the princesses' aunt had gone underground after sneaking out of a mental ward where she'd been held for her own protection.

He moved to stand behind Alessandra, resting one hand on her shoulder, as if she were his touchstone. Alessandra looked up at him briefly, their gazes connecting.

Eloise had to look away, heart pounding uncomfortably against her sternum. She was happy for Alessandra, really she was. But seeing how deeply her sister was loved was a stark reminder of everything Eloise didn't have.

And never would.

She forced herself to concentrate on Gideon's words. "...we'll add a dozen guards for the grounds and another half dozen to check in the guests. Do you think that'll be enough men that it won't slow down traffic into the church?"

"Gideon, is that really necessary?" Alessandra asked. "We don't want the guests to feel as though they are going through security at an airport."

"There haven't been any credible threats, even with Aunty Beatrice on the lam," Mia said.

Gideon shot her a look. "If we let our guard down, we'll be vulnerable."

Eloise tuned them out. Her gaze drifted to the hallway. Father had promised to come down for a bit for family time, but it was already half an hour past his usual time.

Father's nurse stuck her head around the doorway and shook her head slightly.

Father wasn't coming.

The others didn't notice. Mia's husband Ethan had joined her on the sofa, and they spoke together quietly, heads bent close together. Alessandra and Gideon continued to argue, though Eloise knew Gideon was only concerned for his soon-to-be wife. Alessandra would relent, because she knew the same thing.

Eloise couldn't help the jealousy that speared

through her.

It was a ridiculous emotion, one she wished she could eradicate.

Father was dying. There was no disguising the way his health had declined in the past few weeks. And while her sisters were wrapped up in their own lives with new husbands, Eloise remained alone and would soon have the pressure of ruling the kingdom on her shoulders entirely.

A kingdom of citizens who despised her. Some refused to look at her when she made public appearances.

Wild, hot emotion welled up inside her, and before she realized what she was doing, Eloise was on her feet.

"Enough," she screamed.

Mia jumped. The room went silent. Gideon's hand closed over Alessandra's shoulder protectively.

"None of your petty problems matter," she fumed. She didn't really mean the words but couldn't stop the audible flow of emotions.

Mia blinked, her eyes now glistening.

Before she could do any more damage, Eloise rushed from the room.

She ran through the castle's stone halls, brushing past a housekeeper before ducking through one of the servant's halls and out into the salty sea breeze on the private beach.

She gulped in breath after breath of the briny air, but it didn't help calm her roiling emotions.

It wouldn't be long now. Alessandra and Mia put

up with her outbursts because they wanted to stay close to Father as his health declined. Once he was gone, what reason did they have to stay with their monster of a sister?

Soon she would end up all alone, alone with her beastly temper and what staff she could keep on.

She hated herself. Hated that she couldn't change things. Hated the scars that defined her life and had for years.

She'd wanted what her sisters had. Desperately, throughout her lonely teen years, she wanted someone to love her.

But who could ever love a beastly princess like her?

THE TOAD PRINCE

ABOUT THE AUTHOR

USA Today bestselling author Lacy Williams works in a hostile environment (read: four kids age 7 and under). In spite of this, she has somehow managed to be a hybrid author since 2011, publishing 34 books & novellas. Lacy's books have finaled in the *RT Book Reviews* Reviewers' Choice Awards (2012, 2013, & 2014), the Golden Quill and the Booksellers Best Award. She is a member of American Christian Fiction Writers, Romance Writers of America and Novelists Inc.

Made in the USA
Monee, IL
28 March 2021